Puffin Books
A HOUSE INSIDE OUT

Born in 1933, Penelope Lively spent her childhood in Egypt. She did not go to school until she was twelve, when her family moved to England and Penelope was sent to a boarding school in Sussex. She then went to Oxford. In 1957 she married Jack Lively, who is Emeritus Professor of Politics at Warwick University. They have a daughter, and a son, and four grandchildren.

Penelope Lively's first children's novel, *Astercote*, was published in 1970. Since then she has written eighteen books for children, two of which have won awards. In 1974 she won the Carnegie Medal for *The Ghost of Thomas Kempe* and in 1977 she won the Whitbread Award for *A Stitch in Time*.

Of her nine adult books, *The Road To Lichfield* and *According to Mark* were shortlisted for the Booker Prize in 1977 and 1984 respectively and *Moon Tiger* won the prize in 1987.

Penelope Lively now lives in North Oxfordshire and in London

A
HOUSE
INSIDE
OUT

by
Penelope Lively

Illustrated by David Parkins

PUFFIN BOOKS

PUFFIN BOOKS

Published by the Penguin Group
Penguin Books Ltd, 27 Wrights Lane, London W8 5TZ, England
Penguin Putnam Inc., 375 Hudson Street, New York, New York 10014, USA
Penguin Books Australia Ltd, Ringwood, Victoria, Australia
Penguin Books Canada Ltd, 10 Alcorn Avenue, Toronto, Ontario, Canada M4V 3B2
Penguin Books (NZ) Ltd, 182–190 Wairau Road, Auckland 10, New Zealand

Penguin Books Ltd, Registered Offices: Harmondsworth, Middlesex, England

First published by André Deutsch 1987
Published in Puffin Books 1989
13 15 17 19 20 18 16 14

Text copyright © Penelope Lively, 1987
Illustrations copyright © David Parkins, 1987
All rights reserved

Printed in England by Clays Ltd, St Ives plc
Set in Souvenir Light

CONTENTS

1 LOST DOG   1

2 THE MICE, THE TEA-POT AND THE BALL
     OF STRING   9

3 NAT AND THE GREAT BATH CLIMB   21

4 THE RACING PIGEON AND LONDON ZOO   31

5 SAM AND THE HONDA RIDE   40

6 NAT AND THE SPIDER BATTLE   51

7 WILLIE AND THE GREAT HOLE   60

8 SAM AND THE MOUSE MANSION   68

9 THE SPIDER AND THE PEARL   78

10 SAM, MR DIXON'S HANDKERCHIEF, AND
     THE LATE-NIGHT FILM   86

11 WILLIE, THE HAMBURGER AND
     THE BUS-RIDE   95

Chapter One

LOST DOG

Dogs are odd. They are animals, no doubt about that; but to other animals they often seem like offshoots of human beings. This was certainly true of the dog at Fifty-four Pavilion Road, a rough-haired white terrier called Willie. The other creatures in the house thought Willie a helpless fellow because he depended on the Dixon family for food and a roof over his head. Mind, in the case of the mice this could have been said of them also, but I suppose they would have retorted that at least they risked life and limb to get their meals whereas Willie had his handed to him in a bowl. But the real difference is one of outlook rather than the getting of food and shelter. Dogs tend to take a human point of view; they even behave, up to a point, like people.

Willie loved Mrs. Dixon. In fact, he didn't just love Mrs. Dixon — he adored and worshipped her. He was polite to the rest of the family, but it was Mrs. Dixon who was the centre of his world. He had a healthy respect for Mr. Dixon, and he put up with the children — Julie who was nine and Andy who was seven. He had rather mixed feelings about the baby, since he was jealous of him and suspected (rightly, I'm afraid) that Mrs. Dixon loved the baby more than she loved him. But most of Willie's time was spent trailing around after Mrs. Dixon, moping if she wasn't there, and admiring her when she was. He would sit in the kitchen, or the sitting room or wherever she happened to be and croon to her in dog language which of course Mrs. Dixon neither heard nor understood.

"Oh, you are so beautiful," he would sing, "you are so beautiful and so wise and so clever. There is no one like you. I will do anything for you. You are the sun and the moon and I want to live all by myself with you for ever and ever . . ."

It was just as well that Mrs. Dixon, who was a down-to-earth, no nonsense sort of person, was deaf to all this. She was fond of Willie, very fond, though she told him off for being greedy and lazy and always getting underfoot so that she was constantly falling over him.

"It's not me that's underfoot," Willie would grumble, "It's you who are overdog. But I forgive you because you are so wonderful and I admire you and adore you and if you want to step on me just go right ahead and do so."

The Dixons had got Willie when he was young from the RSPCA as an unwanted dog. Perhaps this was why

Willie was so devoted to Mrs. Dixon; she had thought he looked pathetic and said, "Let's have that one." And so it had all begun. And now Willie was, in dog terms, middle-aged, but he still thought Mrs. Dixon was his mother and his rescuer and his benefactor and sang to her daily of his feelings and howled every time she went out. "Alo-o-o-ne," he would wail. "She has left me alone again and I am wretched and she is cruel and she doesn't love me and I am all al-o-o-o-one." After about five minutes he would get tired of this, find himself a nice warm comfortable place and sleep soundly till she came back again.

One Sunday the Dixons all went out to a wild-life park. Since wild-life parks do not welcome dogs Willie had to be left behind. Mrs. Dixon put out a very large meal for him so that there would be no question of him getting hungry if they were late back. Willie watched her do this with an expression of abject misery that said, quite distinctly, that he thought her unfeeling and insensitive to imagine for a moment that he would be able to eat a thing, deserted and abandoned and unloved. Mrs. Dixon told him briskly that he'd be fine. The Dixons left the house, locked the door, got into the car and drove off. Willie howled for exactly five minutes, then stopped, found that he was actually feeling a little peckish after all, went to his bowl and wolfed down half a tin of dog food and a handful of biscuits in thirty seconds flat.

"Creep!" said Sam, the father of the mouse family whose home was at the bottom of a box of old newspapers under the stairs. He had come out for a quick day-time forage around the kitchen.

"Mind your own business!" snarled Willie. He felt comfortably sleepy now, after that extra large meal, and was wondering where to curl up and have a good long snooze. The door to the sitting room was shut, which was a nuisance — he was specially fond of the sofa.

Sam whisked up onto the dresser, discovered that Mrs. Dixon had left out the packet of dog biscuits, nipped inside and helped himself to one. "Your trouble," he continued, with his mouth full of biscuit, "is that you've no sense of get up and go. No push. No oomph and zoom. You just hang about — wait for it to happen . . ."

"Leave those biscuits alone," spluttered Willie.

"No way," said Sam. "Proves my point. All things come to them as helps themselves. Now me, I go out and look for it."

Willie glared. "Belt up, can't you."

Sam shrugged. "Now if you spoke nicely to me I might see my way to chucking you down an extra biscuit."

But Willie was no longer hungry. He was extremely full and very sleepy. He couldn't be bothered to quarrel with Sam any more. He pottered out of the kitchen and up the stairs, in search of a good sleeping place. He looked in the children's room, which was a muddle of toys and did not interest him. The bathroom was boring also. But then he discovered to his joy the Dixons' bedroom door had been left not properly closed. He gave it a good shove with his nose and went in. Oh, wonderful! If there was one place in the house that Willie preferred above all it was Mr. and Mrs. Dixon's bed; it was the one place, also, that was absolutely forbidden. But here he was, all alone, no one would discover him — as soon as he heard them coming back he could dash down the stairs and go through the welcome home routine as hard as he could. No one would know where he had been.

He jumped up on the bed and shuffled around a bit to make himself a nice nest. Then it occurred to him that he could do better than that. He scrabbled at the cover, got his nose underneath, heaved up the sheet and blankets and wriggled right down to the bottom of the bed. It was dark, private, and smelled gloriously of Mrs. Dixon. It was paradise. Dogs, long ago and far back in their ancestries, were den animals, which is why they still like creeping under the furniture and into cosy, hidden places.

Willie had found the perfect den. He gave a great sigh of contentment and sank into a deep, deep sleep.

Towards the end of the afternoon the Dixons returned. Willie, buried in the bottom of the bed, heard nothing. He was still sleeping off that extra large meal. He slept and slept.

The Dixons searched for Willie. They searched the

whole house. Mrs. Dixon popped her head round the bedroom door, saw that the bed was a little untidy but thought that the children had been jumping on it. She came downstairs again and an almighty argument broke out between Mr. and Mrs. Dixon as to whether or not Mr. Dixon had seen to it that Willie was back inside the house before they left.

"You knew I was busy getting the picnic ready," scolded Mrs. Dixon. "I told you to put him out in the garden for five minutes and then see he was safe in the kitchen. You must have left him outside."

"And he's gone off and got run over," wailed Julie Dixon.

"Or been stolen," cried Andy Dixon.

"I tell you he was in the kitchen," shouted their father.

"He can't have been," snapped Mrs. Dixon.

"And I tell you he was," bawled her husband.

The argument died down, as family arguments will. Whoever had done what, Willie was no longer there, which was the important thing. The children were sent to ask all the neighbours if anyone had seen anything of him. Mr. Dixon drove around in the car, looking for him. There was nothing to be seen or heard of a squarish, rather overweight rough-haired white terrier.

Mrs. Dixon rang up the police, who were polite and took down details but made it clear that they could not, as she suggested, put several men on the job immediately. They did, they gently pointed out, have other things to do apart from looking for people's lost dogs. Mrs. Dixon, by now, was quite distraught; she put the phone down and turned on Mr. Dixon again.

The entire Dixon family were by now squabbling. Mr. Dixon — poor fellow — was blamed for having left Willie outside, however much he went on insisting that he hadn't. The children kept bursting into tears as they imagined the dreadful things that must have happened.

6

Mrs. Dixon, who just felt guilty in general, was snapping at everyone. Eventually she said that they had had a long day and everyone was overtired and had better go to bed. She drove the children into the bath, scurried them through their supper and tucked them up. Then she and her husband watched the news — there were no headlines, as she felt there ought to be, about "All police leave was cancelled in the Birmingham area this evening as the search intensified for a small white terrier named Willie . . ." At last they locked the front door, turned out the lights and went upstairs.

They undressed. Mrs. Dixon used the bathroom. She came back to the bedroom and took off the bedcover. She said, "The children have been messing about in here again — just look at the state this is in." Mrs. Dixon folded the cover, put it on the chair, kicked off her slippers and slid down into the bed.

Her feet landed on something warm and hairy. She shot backwards with a yell.

Willie crawled out from under the bedclothes, blinking and looking somewhat rumpled. He saw Mrs. Dixon standing beside the bed in her nightdress, began to fling himself joyfully at her, remembered with horror that he had no business to be where he was, panicked and tried to dive under the bed, where he stuck fast.

Mr. Dixon hauled him out by the back legs. The children, woken by the commotion, came rushing in. Willie rolled over on his back and cringed at everyone, rolling his eyes till the whites showed. "Don't beat me," he begged. "Don't murder me. It was all a ghastly mistake. I didn't mean to. I swear I never will again. If you weren't so cruel and horrible, leaving me all on my own without a bite to eat and those blessed mice making fun of me, it would never have happened."

Willie wasn't beaten. Some stern words were said, especially by Mr. Dixon. Willie was marched smartly

downstairs and put to bed in the kitchen. He never got into the Dixons' bed again; not, I'm afraid, because he had learned a lesson but because Mrs. Dixon took special care not to leave the door of the bedroom open.

8

Chapter Two

THE MICE, THE TEA-POT AND THE BALL OF STRING

There were three different families of mice at Fifty-four Pavilion Road. One lived in the back of the airing cupboard, another under the sitting room floorboards and a third in the bottom of a box of old newspapers under the stairs. They were all related — cousins and sisters-in-law and aunts and grandmothers — but each family returned to its own nest by day. At night, though, everyone hunted for food throughout the house, collecting all the bits and pieces people never miss: the cornflakes under the baby's chair, the crumbs in the toaster, the scraps of fat stuck to the cooker. They exchanged news and gossip, swopped a scrap of bacon rind for a shred of baked potato skin or sat by the kitchen boiler warming themselves and nagging the children.

Young mice are brought up with rules and warnings which are drummed into them from the moment they leave the nest. The rules are added to or altered according to the times, but by and large have been passed on from generation to generation. They go something like this:

DON'T SLEEP IN THE DIRTY CLOTHES BASKET
DON'T TEASE THE DOG
NEVER EAT MATCHES
BE PLEASANT TO BABIES

DON'T GET INTO THE BACK OF THE TELE-
VISION: GREAT-UNCLE THOMAS DID THAT
AND WISHED HE HADN'T

DON'T FOOL AROUND WITH EMPTY MILK
BOTTLES; YOU MAY FALL IN

OVENS ARE FOR COOKING: COOKED MOUSE
IS UNCOMFORTABLE

YOUR PARENTS ARE ALWAYS RIGHT

And young mice, just like human children, turn a
deaf ear to a good deal of this and occasionally regret it
(like great-uncle Thomas, who was a teenager at the
time). Teasing the dog, indeed, was a long-standing
tradition, as was a game called Scooter which involved
racing each other round the lavatory seat — more
dangerous by far than any milk bottle. All young mice
dared one another to climb to the top of the sitting
room curtains; all of them, at one time or another,
explored the oven and the inside of the vacuum
cleaner and slid down the big lampshade behind the
sofa. They fought to be first into the toaster each night,
where there was a lovely harvest of crumbs for those small
enough to squeeze between the wires and swing hand
over hand down to the shiny tray at the bottom. In the
early mornings they played chicken in the bedroom
waste-paper basket — hiding in the bottom until the
very moment the Dixons started to wake up; those
who were rash and stayed too long had to huddle there
under kleenex and hair-combings while the floor shook
as the Dixons tramped terrifyingly above and around
them.

Each mouse family had tales of adventure and
daring. Some of these, over the years, had become
rather highly coloured. There was the ancestor who
was said to have used a handkerchief to parachute
from the landing down into the hall. The airing
cupboard mice had a legend of a member of their
family who was imprisoned in a biscuit tin when

someone put the lid on while he was inside it; he ate a
pound of Tea-time Fancies over the next five days and
sprang out three sizes bigger when the lid was taken off
again.

No doubt there was some truth in these stories, but
mice, like humans, like to spin a good yarn and some of
them, undoubtedly, had become a little wild. Mother
mice liked to threaten their children with accounts of
disaster: the young mouse who had fallen into the
goldfish bowl and been gobbled up; another who drank
blackcurrant syrup and turned pink; the youngest
child who fell asleep inside the sewing-machine and
was hemmed into a curtain.

All such stories start somewhere; most of these were lost in times past — they had happened "Back when I was a girl . . ." or "When my grandmother was alive . . ." or "More years ago than I care to think . . ." But presumably all had their beginnings in some real event. Such, perhaps, as the drama of the teapot, which took place precisely as I shall tell it.

It was a night like any other. The Dixon family went to bed; Mr. Dixon turned off the bedside light; downstairs the television was silent, the gas fire in the sitting room ticked from time to time as it grew cold, the light from the street-lamp splashed through the window onto the floor.

The Stair mice were first into the kitchen. The father, Sam by name and a decent enough fellow though a bit of a loud-mouth in the opinion of some, sent his children into the toaster and shinned up a chair-back onto the kitchen table, where Mrs. Dixon, as usual, had left breakfast already laid. The cereal packet was an unopened one, so there was nothing doing there (he could, of course, have nibbled a hole in the corner as easy as winking, but sensible mice do not leave traces so obvious as to invite a whole programme of traps and cats). He pottered around for a while, shouted instructions to his wife, who was dealing with an apple-core one of the Dixon children had dropped behind the rubbish-bin, and greeted various friends and relations who were now appearing from the rest of the house.

The Airing Cupboard mice had some interesting gossip and the Sitting Room mice were complaining that Mr. Dixon had had Sportsnight on the telly turned up full blast right above their nest under the floorboards. "My head's splitting!" wailed the mother. "The Grand National crashing round and round over my head . . ."

Sam's attention strayed to the teapot. Mrs. Dixon

had left the lid off, which was unusual. She was also in the habit of putting the tea in the pot the night before, all ready to brew up first thing in the morning. Sam was particularly fond of tea, which mice will chew much like humans at one time used to chew tobacco. He swarmed up the teapot by way of the handle and looked inside; yes, a nice little mound of Typhoo. He dropped down on top of it.

Upstairs, Mrs. Dixon was lying awake. The longer she lay awake the more she had a nasty feeling she'd left the gas-fire on. The nasty feeling turned into an even nastier one that she could smell burning. She

13

tried nudging her husband, who was comfortably snoring. At last she sighed, got out of bed, put on her dressing-gown and slippers and crept downstairs.

The mice, at the first sound of the bedroom door opening, shot between cracks in the floorboards, under the cooker and behind the sink. Sam scrabbled for a moment at the slippery sides of the teapot and decided to stay where he was.

Mrs. Dixon went into the sitting room, saw the fire was off, sniffed around, came into the kitchen, put the light on, and noted that all was well. She picked up an apple core that was lying in the middle of the floor and popped it in the bin; glancing at the table, she noticed that the lid was off the teapot and put it on. Then she turned out the light, went upstairs and back to bed where she fell asleep within a few minutes.

The mice came out again. Sam's wife, Doris, called her children out from the toaster, where they had remained in hiding, counted them, and then searched unsuccessfully for her apple-core. After a few minutes it occurred to her that she didn't know where her husband was — and then suddenly all the mice became aware of Sam's faint cries coming from within the teapot.

Everyone swarmed up onto the table. They stood around the teapot and from within Sam's cries became a positive roar of distress. "Keep calm, dear," cried his wife. "Take deep breaths and keep absolutely calm." I think I should not record Sam's reply to this.

"Well," said the oldest mouse of all, a grandfather who claimed to remember the occasion of great-uncle Thomas and the television. "This is a nice how-d'you do."

"Get out through the spout, father," advised one of Sam's children, who was almost small enough to do so. Sam's reply to this cannot be repeated either.

Sam's mother, who did not often get the chance to

14

criticize him nowadays, said that he should have known better in the first place, teapots were always unreliable and Sam had been a greedy fellow since he was so high and if she'd told him once she'd told him a thousand times — chew tea and your teeth'll drop out.

"Shut up!" bawled Sam from within the teapot.

"And don't you talk to me like that," said his mother.

"Just keep quite calm!" wailed his wife.

The mice crowded around the teapot. What on earth was to be done? The teapot was enormous; it towered over them, its curving slippery sides decorated with a pattern of green leaves, its rim chipped where a young Dixon had once knocked it over. The mice considered what would happen in the morning. Mrs. Dixon would come down, she would put the kettle on, the kettle would come to the boil, she would take the lid off the teapot, pick up the kettle and . . .

"Oh, poor father!" cried the children.

"Get me out of here!" howled Sam, not calm at all.

It was the chip in the rim of the teapot that gave them the idea. Someone pointed out that if only they could push it over, the lid would fall off . . . But of course it was far too heavy for them to push over, even everyone heaving and shoving together. If on the other hand they could tip it off the edge of the table . . . And at that moment one of them spotted the ball of string with which Mr. Dixon had been tying up a parcel the night before and had left lying on the dresser — and the idea was born.

It could be done. Possibly. The thing to do was to chew off a length of string, thread it through the handle of the teapot, hang the string down over the edge of the table onto the floor, get everyone down there and then all pull, as in a tug of war.

They explained to Sam. Either the teapot would break or the lid would roll off.

Sam was silent for a moment. "What about me?" he demanded.

"You jump out, dear," said his wife.

"Of course I jump out," snapped Sam. "S'pose I've been broken too?"

It would be like flying, they told him, only quicker. It would be quite an experience. The children said they wished it was them.

Sam, within the teapot, sat on the pile of tea (one thing was for sure — he'd never chew a tea-leaf again, never in his life) and looked miserably at the curving walls of his prison. He had a sinking feeling inside him already. "All right," he muttered, "get on with it."

The other mice hardly heard him. They were already busy. One party climbed up the dresser, unreeled a length of string, bit it off and trailed it up onto the table. They passed one end through the handle of the teapot and then let the two ends fall to the ground. Then all the mice gathered on the floor and pulled both ends of the string at once. The teapot shifted slightly and Sam gave a nervous squeak. "Watch it! I'm not ready!"

"Have you out of there in a jiffy, mate," cried his friends.

"Hang on a minute," pleaded Sam.

"What's the problem?"

"No problem," said Sam. "No hurry either. Just take it easy."

"What's the matter, dear?" enquired his wife.

"Nothing's the matter," snarled Sam. "I'm having a rest, aren't I?"

"Father's afraid," said his youngest child.

"No, I'm not," snapped Sam. "Another word from you and I'll belt you when I get out."

"Father *is* afraid," said the youngest child, more quietly.

But the mice were by now quite carried away by their cleverness and skill. Everyone was crowded

around the two ends of string, ready to pull. The father of the Sitting Room mice appointed himself leader: "When I shout HEAVE! — everyone start pulling. You all set, Sam?"

"Hold on a minute!" cried Sam, from the teapot: —

"Just want to have a few minutes to . . ."

But no one heard him. "HEAVE!" cried the leader. They all braced themselves against the kitchen floor, from largest to smallest, and pulled for all they were worth. One or two of the smallest and youngest lost their footing, fell over backwards and hastily scrambled up again. The teapot rocked.

"Help!" cried Sam. "Look here — I've changed my mind. I reckon I'll just stop here. Maybe if we . . ."

But his words were lost. "HEAVE!" roared the leader again. The mice strained and heaved. The teapot lurched. "Here we go!" cried the leader.

"Here you come, Sam! Mind your heads everyone!"

The teapot tottered and tipped. "NO!" shrieked Sam. "Hold it, you lot . . . Stop!"

But it was too late. He felt the teapot go over onto one side; he slid this way and that; tea showered all over him. And then his stomach was somewhere way over his head, in fact he had left it behind altogether, he was falling down . . . down . . . down . . . until WHAM! . . . his prison flew apart and there he was sitting on the kitchen floor, juddering all over and with his ears ringing. And all round him were his family, friends and relations, most of them upside down, having fallen on their backs when the string slackened and the teapot came hurtling off the table.

The teapot was no more. At least it was in half a dozen pieces. And there was the most appalling noise going on; Willie the dog had been woken by the crash, had leapt out of his basket and was barking fit to burst. "Burglars!" he yelled. "Masked men! Raiders! Red alert!" The mice picked themselves up and began to scurry for cover. Willie caught sign of them, realised his mistake and went on barking since it now seemed the only thing to do.

The bedroom door opened. Mr. Dixon came thundering downstairs. The baby woke up and started to cry. Mrs. Dixon rushed to the baby. The Dixon children came padding down after their father, hoping for thrills.

Mr. Dixon switched on the kitchen light. There stood Willie, still barking frantically, and there on the floor was the broken teapot. Mr. Dixon swore at Willie and advanced on him with raised hand.

"I didn't do it," whined Willie. He laid his ears back and crawled on his belly towards Mr. Dixon. "Honest. Cross my heart. It was those blessed mice, and just wait till I get my paws on one of them, I'll give them what for, I'll teach them a lesson." But a fine lot of good that did him, since of course Mr. Dixon couldn't understand a word.

The Dixon children, seeing their father about to start walloping the dog, rushed forward pleading for mercy. Mr. Dixon gave Willie a few token clouts and fetched a dustpan and brush to sweep up the broken teapot. The children were sent back to bed. Mrs. Dixon appeared, holding the baby, who was still howling, and wanted to know what was going on.

The baby looked over his mother's shoulder and saw Sam, who was hiding under a fold in the rug. Sam was feeling extremely dizzy and every bone in his body ached. The baby stopped crying and smiled. Sam waggled his whiskers at it. The baby smiled more and flapped his hands at Sam.

"Ssh!" said Sam. "Not a word, eh! You be a good lad and one of these days I'll tell you a story about how I went flying in a teapot. Right?" And the baby gurgled and smiled and presently Mr. and Mrs. Dixon turned the kitchen light out, closed the door and went upstairs to bed again.

"Right," snarled Willie, "now let's be having yer . . ."

But the mice had gone, even Sam. They had slipped off to their nests by the highways and byways that only they knew about, the back alleys of a house that human beings know nothing of — the cracks and crannies and spaces below floorboards and behind skirting boards. And Sam was already forgetting his aches and pains and starting to put the polish on what was going to be a famous family story of courage and daring, in which he, of course, was the hero.

Chapter Three

NAT AND THE GREAT BATH CLIMB

The life of a young wood-louse is a very different matter to that of a young mouse. Mice are free and easy creatures compared to wood-lice. Young mice are warned and scolded, but they also get away with a good deal, since their parents are skittish creatures themselves who enjoy a bit of fun and like to get the best out of life. Wood-lice are another matter; their way of life is as stiff and awkward as their appearance. They have an outlook on life which is all their own — as indeed do most of us, but people tend to ignore that in the case of something with a top view like a very small armadillo and fourteen legs, which is why Mrs. Dixon was so silly as to scream whenever she saw one. The wood-lice had to put up with a great deal more from Mrs. Dixon — and the rest of the Dixons — than she did from them.

The wood-lice at Fifty-four Pavilion Road lived in several large colonies. They preferred damp and murky places — the corner behind the sink where a dripping tap had made an area of moist and flaking plaster, the cupboard in the cloakroom where mildew grew on the Dixons' winter boots, the waste-pipe of the bath.

The waste-pipe was considered a particularly attractive habitat. Admittedly two or three times each day a Niagara falls of soapy water came hurtling down and many a wood-louse had hurtled down with it and had to climb

up again some fifteen feet from the drain outside. But wood-lice are sturdy uncomplaining creatures and they took this as part of the price one had to pay for a home that was forever dark, forever damp and forever undisturbed by mops and vacuum-cleaners. The waste-pipe had in fact several cracks and faulty joins through which they could climb out into the wall when threatened by bathwater. More than that, it gave them a magnificent opportunity to do what wood-lice do.

Wood-lice colonies are governed by Chief Wood-lice, who are stern and ancient creatures with whiskers of immense length. Young wood-lice are kept under the most strict control by their elders; indeed they are quite literally trampled on until large enough to hold their own. Wood-lice are not creatures who go in much for expressing themselves or being original or striking out; one wood-louse acts and thinks much like another and this is the way the old wood-lice want to keep it.

From time to time the Chief Wood-louse would call the whole colony together for a meeting. The object of this meeting was for the Chief Wood-louse to lecture the newest generation of young wood-lice, who were allowed to attend as soon as their whiskers were three millimetres long, which meant they were grown-up.

The hero of this story, who was called Nat, came to his first such meeting when he was three weeks old — which in human terms is about eighteen years. The young wood-lice sat in a row in the front, feeling important but nervous, while their parents and aunts and uncles crowded behind them and the Chief Wood-louse took up a position in front.

The Chief Wood-louse looked sternly down at the assembled crowd and began to speak. "We are gathered together today," he said, "to remind ourselves of the purpose of life." He glared at the young wood-lice. "And what is the purpose of life?" The young wood-lice, who knew they were not supposed to answer, gazed at him respectfully.

"The purpose of life is to climb up the side of the bath. That is what we are here for. That is why we were born. No one has ever succeeded. But the purpose of life is to try. Each and every one of us. Your turn has now come. Your mothers and fathers have tried before

23

you. Some brave spirits have tried several times. All have failed."

There was a silence. The young wood-lice gazed at the Chief Wood-louse and felt even more nervous and important. All except Nat, who was the youngest and smallest and had been in trouble most of his life for asking too many questions. Nat was thinking.

"You will make your attempts turn and turn about, starting with the eldest. Each of you will fail, but will have made a glorious attempt, you will then have your names inscribed on the Roll of Honour."

The young wood-lice went quite pink with pride and excitement, all except Nat, who raised one of his fourteen legs. "Please, sir," he said, "why do we have to climb up the side of the bath?"

There was a gasp of horror from the crowd of wood-lice. Nat's mother fainted clean away; his father bent his head in shame.

The Chief Wood-louse stared at Nat. His whiskers twitched in fury. "WHAT DID YOU SAY?"

Nat cleared his throat and repeated, politely and clearly, "Why do we have to climb up the side of the bath?"

The Chief Wood-louse huffed and puffed; his little black eyes bulged; he creaked with indignation. "BECAUSE IT'S THERE!" he roared and there was a rustle of agreement from the crowd of wood-lice. Some of the youngsters turned to look reprovingly at Nat. His mother recovered from her faint and moaned that she would never get over the disgrace, never.

Nat sat tight. He said nothing more. He kept his thoughts to himself.

The young wood-lice made their assaults upon the side of the bath alone. Each in turn would struggle up through the plug-hole and vanish from sight. Some while later — much later, sometimes — they would crawl back down again in a state of exhaustion. One or two said with shy pride that they had got six inches before they fell back. The unluckiest of all did not crawl back into the plug-hole but tumbled back in a torrent of water, having been spotted by Mrs. Dixon. One after another they tried, and one after another they returned, beaten but content. When it came to Nat's turn his parents and relatives gathered round him and told him severely that this was his chance to make a man of himself and become exactly like everyone else. "Try hard," they told him, "and fail magnificently, and we shall be proud of you."

Nat looked upwards. Bright light, which hurt his eyes, came through the plug-hole. He hauled himself up and out. It was dazzlingly bright out there and, for a few moments, he could see nothing but the glitter of the chrome circle on which he was standing. He felt terrifyingly exposed. Then he looked round and saw the whole immense smooth white length of the bath reaching away before him. It was even more enormous than people had said — it seemed to go on for ever, and if he looked to right or to left its sides towered upwards, first sloping and then absolutely sheer, up and up as far as you could see.

Nat walked out a few steps. It was very slippery. Even on the flat his legs slithered about. He toiled across to one side and gradually the smooth hard surface began to slope. He slithered even more. He slithered back to where he had started.

He looked at those white cliffs. Of course you couldn't climb them. That was the whole point.

He struggled a little way up the slope again. Then he lost his grip and rolled down to the bottom.

Stuff this, thought Nat, I'm not carrying on with this lark. He sat down where he was and looked around him. The bath was a very boring place, he decided — either flat white or steep white and with nothing to look at. There was one of Mr. Dixon's hairs, which to Nat was like a length of rope but not very interesting. There was also a grain of Mrs. Dixon's bath-salts which he tried to eat; it tasted nasty so he spat it out. He thought about going back down the plug-hole; he could say — truthfully enough — that he had tried to climb up the side of the bath, and failed. He could have his name inscribed on the Roll of Honour, like everyone else. The idea of that was as boring as the scenery of the bath.

"Well!" said a voice. "Get on with it, then! Strive and struggle! Press on! Wear yourself out! That's what you're here for, isn't it?"

Nat looked all round. He could see no one.

"What's the matter?" continued the voice. "Where's your grit and determination?"

Nat looked up. Far above him, on the distant heights of the right hand side of the bath, he saw some legs. The legs twitched, took a few neat steps downwards and a large spider came into view.

"Go on," said the spider, "climb. Give me something to laugh at."

"I'm not going to," said Nat. "There's no point. We can't."

The spider let out a length of thread and swung itself down until it was hanging halfway down the side of the bath. "Good grief! The first one of you with his head screwed on right. Too right you can't. I, on the other hand . . ." It gripped the side of the bath for a moment, and then swarmed up its thread and re-appeared at the top. "Neat, eh?"

"Terrific," said Nat. "What is it like up there?"

"Truth to tell," said the spider, "there's not all that much to it. Quite a nice view. Come and see."

Nat stared. "But . . ." he began.

"Wait," ordered the spider. It raised its two rear legs and began to spin a great length of thread, which streamed out and came floating down until the end of it reached Nat in the bottom of the bath. "Take hold," instructed the spider. "Hang on tight."

Nat gripped the thread, which was sticky and felt slightly elastic but strong. The spider became very busy with its eight legs and Nat felt himself being slowly towed up the slope of the bath. He clung on for dear life. The spider continued to reel in the thread and Nat found himself rising up the sheer white wall. He swung around alarmingly and once or twice was bumped against the side. "Fend off," advised the spider. "Use your feet. Not much further."

Up went Nat. He did not dare look down. Once, he thought; I am doing what no other wood-louse has ever done.

"There!" said the spider. "Piece of cake, isn't it?"

Nat found himself standing on a white cliff-top. He walked to the far edge and looked out into the bathroom, which, since wood-lice are better at smelling than seeing, appeared to him as a dizzying scene of distant and colourful blurs. There was a terrifying drop down to a great expanse of green (which was in fact the bathmat) and an overwhelming smell of flowers (which came from Mrs. Dixon's Country Garden talcum powder). I am where no other wood-louse has ever been, thought Nat.

"Mind," said the spider, 'once you're here there's not a lot to do. One just kind of hangs out for a bit and then goes down again. Personally I find the top of the standard lamp in the sitting room more exhilarating. But you wouldn't know about that."

"No," said Nat. He didn't think he wanted to either.

"Anyway, you'll have something to tell the folks back home."

'No," said Nat. "I can't possibly tell them. This isn't the way you're supposed to do it."

"Well, suit yourself." The spider began grooming itself with its two front legs. Nat noticed that on one

side it had two legs that were very much shorter than the others.

"What happened to your legs?" he asked. He had often seen spiders before but had never been on such close terms with one and, as we know, he was fond of asking questions.

"Nosy fellow, aren't you?" said the spider. "I had a slight difference of opinion with a friend, as it happens. Quite good fun at the time." It was a ferocious looking creature; you'd do well to stay on the right side of it, Nat thought.

"How about a quick spin down to the bathmat and up to the laundry basket?" continued the spider.

Nat thanked it but said he thought he ought to be getting back now. The spider spun a short length of thread, Nat took hold of it, and the spider lowered him slowly over the side and down into the bath again. When he got to the bottom Nat gave the thread a tug,

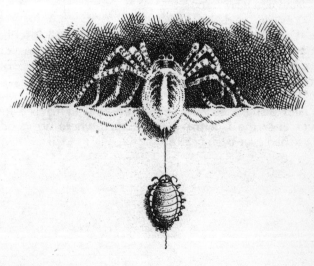

as he had been instructed, let go of it, and the spider reeled it back in again. Then it peered down over the edge and called, "Well, cheerio then. See you around, I daresay."

"Cheerio," called Nat, "and thanks very much. I enjoyed it."

"Don't mention it," said the spider. "Take care. Don't do anything I wouldn't do."

Nat trudged back down the length of the bath. He slithered across the chrome of the plug-hole and down into the dark, homely hole. He crawled down the damp, familiar pipe and when he got to the first bend there was a reception committee of wood-lice waiting for him, headed by the Chief Wood-louse.

"You have tried to climb up the side of the bath?" said the Chief Wood-louse, in his most stern and dreadful tones.

"Yes, sir," said Nat.

"And you have failed?"

"Yes, sir," said Nat.

"Then," said the Chief Wood-louse "I shall inscribe your name on the Roll of Honour. From now on you are exactly the same as every other wood-louse. Be proud of it."

"Yes, sir," said Nat.

And being a sensible fellow, he kept to himself for ever after the fact that he had been where no wood-louse had ever been before.

Chapter Four

THE RACING PIGEON
AND LONDON ZOO

House mice, especially those more adventurous than the rest, can feel from time to time that they lead dull lives. The daily — or nightly — routine of scavenging in the kitchen, and exploring elsewhere can seem monotonous. The mice at Pavilion Road considered on the whole that the house supplied all they needed, but even so they were fascinated by accounts of the world beyond. Sam, in particular, would creep up to the attic to hear tales told by the racing pigeon, who was a particular friend of his.

The racing pigeon would drop down onto the roof once a month or so, strut around for a while and then slip under the broken tile beside the chimney stack to roost on the rafters. He should not have been doing this, of course. Top-notch racing pigeons head for home and keep going till they get there. This one, though a fine handsome fellow, was no longer in the first division so far as racing was concerned; his owner, an old age pensioner in Barnsley, only went on sending him out as a matter of habit. The pigeon had taken prizes in his day; nowadays, he took his time, dropping off at Pavilion Road for a breather and to impress Sam with tales of another world.

"Knackered, I am," he said, "had the wind against me right the way across the Channel. Blowing a Force Eight gale. I was tempted to hitch a lift on the car ferry, I can tell you."

"But you didn't," said Sam admiringly.

The pigeon snorted. "I'm not a flipping seagull, am I? I couldn't have looked myself in the face. But I tell you, I was never more glad to see Southampton dock."

Sam looked knowing. "You were on the Cherbourg run, then?"

"That's right, son. Always Cherbourg in October. And always we have dodgy weather."

Most racing pigeons, as you probably know, come from the north of England and are sent south by train in wicker baskets, stowed away in the guard's van and taken out at stations far away, sometimes across the channel to France. There, the baskets are opened, the pigeons released and off they go at sixty miles an hour back home to their lofts in Barnsley or Huddersfield or South Shields or wherever. How they do it has never been explained; certainly the Pavilion Road pigeon was not able to do so. "Well," he would say, if pressed, "you just get up there and go, don't you? I mean, you just face the right way and keep on going till you get there."

On this particular run, apparently, he had been blown off course and obliged to land for a while somewhere in Wiltshire. "Shocking, it was. Rain chucking down, a north-easter fit to strip the feathers off you. It reminded me of the time I broke my wing and fetched up in London Zoo. Did I ever tell you about that?"

Sam settled himself down comfortably. "No," he said.

"It was a sou'-wester that time," said the pigeon. "Autumn gale. A proper stinker. I was on the Harwich run. Hook of Holland to Harwich. They opened the baskets at five in the morning and I took one look at the sky and thought, this is going to be a tough one. Clouds hanging low and black with rain; the sort of wind that chucks you around like a leaf. I got up there and you couldn't see a thing. Like flying to nowhere. You just had to get onto automatic pilot and bash on, hoping for the best. I wasn't so lucky. A couple of hours out the clouds were so low I was down to roof height, flying blind, and I went straight into a telegraph pole, slap bang wallop. Next thing I knew I was on the ground. One wing trailing. No way I could take off again. It was raining hard. I seemed to be in some sort of park — roads, pavements, grassy bits, humans walking around, though not that many, on account of the rain. And then I heard the most fearful noise. Enough to make your blood run cold. Know the noise a cat makes at night?"

Sam shuddered and nodded.

"Like that, but louder. And then that stopped but there was a terrible roaring instead. I looked round and suddenly I spotted a creature such as I'd never seen or dreamed of — as big as a house, grey, with legs like tree-trunks and a great thing like a snake hanging down at the front of its head. I thought I must have flown off the face of the earth. There were some other pigeons around — town pigeons, ordinary folk — so I went over to have a word with them and find out where I was. "You're at London Zoo, mate," they said. "Best restaurant in town. Join the club. Get stuck in." And they moved off the cheese sandwich they were scoffing so that I could have a peck, which was decent of them, I suppose, but frankly I've been accustomed to better than that. Only the best grain, my man gives me, back in my loft. None of your pappy white sliced loaf."

The pigeon was referring to the old age pensioner in Barnsley, of course, from whose loft he came. The pensioner thought he owned the pigeon; the pigeon considered that he owned both the man and the loft.

"All the same, I was starving, so I ate a bit and then got under a bench to think things out. I couldn't fly. I'd have to stay put — grounded — till my wing healed, which might take quite a while. I was in danger. Cats. Humans, most of all. I could mix with the other pigeons for as long as I could, but anyone looking hard would soon spot I wasn't one of them. I mean, let's face it, I don't look like any old common or garden town pigeon."

He had a point. Racing pigeons are sleeker and slimmer than ordinary ones — they look like what they are: creatures built for speed. They have fine, white ringed eyes and an alert expression. They also have a neat metal ring around one leg, which gives their number and the loft from which they come. The ring is not very obvious but anyone sharp-eyed would notice it.

"I looked around. And I saw that I was near the most enormous cage for birds you ever saw in your life. It was as big as half a dozen houses put together. There were trees growing inside it, and a great pond, and grass and bushes, and there were birds in there such as I'd never seen. I couldn't believe my eyes. I tell you, there were pink birds with legs like a couple of long sticks. And bright scarlet birds and green ones and others that were all the colours of the rainbow with long trailing tails. And there were ducks and geese with crazy plumage and things that I could see were some kind of pigeon but didn't look like any self-respecting pigeon would care to look. And as I watched I saw a man come and open a wire door and go inside this enormous cage and take in a trolley with every kind of food you can imagine — top-notch stuff, good grain, different things for different kinds of birds, and he chucked all this around and then came out again and shut the door. There they were, safe as houses and a square meal brought in once a day. Right, I thought to myself, that's the place for me. I'll get myself in there and lie low till I'm fit again. Then I'll scarper just as soon as I'm ready.

"It wasn't difficult. I skulked around by the entrance and when the man came again with the trolley of food I nipped in after him. Then I got under a bush till he'd gone, and there I was — safe from cats and people and some good nosh into the bargain. But what a crew they were in there! First of all I could hardly understand a word they said. Jabber jabber jabber in every language under the sun. Mind, some of them had been hatched in the aviary — that was what they called this cage — and spoke proper English. And all they did the whole day long was preen themselves and chatter. Mind,

there wasn't much else for them to do — with everything served up for them on a plate and nothing required but to look pretty and do whatever they did — swim up and down the lake or sit singing in the tops of the trees or jabbering in the bushes. And all the time humans walked around the outside and stared at them."

"Why?" said Sam.

"Why? because that's what places like that are for. Zoos. Aviaries. For humans to look at animals and birds. Mind, it would drive me bananas, but most of that crew in there were so used to it they didn't care, and there were those that were such show-offs they weren't happy unless they had an audience. There was hardly a soul I could have a decent conversation with, either. I did get friendly with one fellow who claimed to be a pigeon, but you should have seen him — bright blue with a yellow tail. Up in Barnsley they wouldn't have given him the time of day, I can tell you."

"What did you do when your wing got better?" asked Sam.

"I'm just getting to that, aren't I? Soon as I felt a bit stronger I tried flying around a bit, to get myself tuned up again. But of course this meant someone — one of those gawping humans — might spot I wasn't one of those crazy foreign birds and make trouble for me. But I had to take the risk — couldn't fly home till I'd got limbered up.

"So I tried to be as inconspicuous as I could — I'd just sit up in a tree and then do a quick swoop to another and then sit quiet again. But I must have been seen because early one morning when I was roosting I came to and found I was being dragged off the perch. I'd been caught in a net at the end of a long pole, by the fellow who used to bring the food in. Pleased as punch, he was. Thought he'd been ever so clever."

"What was he going to do?" asked Sam with interest. "Eat you?"

"Don't be daft! Worse than that. Send me back up to Barnsley, to the loft, that's what he'd have done."

"I thought you wanted to get back?"

The pigeon cocked his head at Sam and gave him a withering look out of one lordly white-ringed eye. *"In a basket? On the train?* What do you take me for? I would have died of shame. You go back to the loft on the wing, or not at all."

"I see," said Sam humbly.

"A basket was just where he did put me. With the lid firmly closed. And he dumped the basket down in some place where there were other animals in cages, looking sorry for themselves. It was the Zoo hospital. I guessed someone was going to come along to look me over and see if I was injured still. So I got myself ready. I peeked out through the cracks in the basket and as soon as a fellow in a white coat came up and opened the basket I shot out before he could lay a hand on me and flew out of his reach to the top of one of the cages.

"A proper commotion there was. All the stuff in the cages — monkeys and that — started screeching and yelling, and the fellow in the white coat grabbed one of those nets on a pole and tried to catch me. But I was too quick for him — I nipped from one place to another and then when someone opened the door to see what all the fuss was about I saw my chance and I was over his head and outside before you could say knife."

"Then what?"

"Then home, of course. Back up to Barnsley, to my man."

"Was he pleased to see you?"

"Was he heck . . . I was three weeks overdue, wasn't I? He'd given me up. Anyway . . ." — the pigeon yawned — " . . . that was just about the worst run I ever had. Except the time I was taken prisoner in a shoe factory. Did I ever tell you about that?"

"No," said Sam eagerly "Go on . . ."

"Another time, son. I need a kip. And then I'll have to

be on my way. Next time I'm passing I'll tell you about that." And he hunched his head down into his shoulder, closed his eyes and went to sleep.

Chapter Five

SAM AND THE HONDA RIDE

The racing pigeon had a bad effect upon Sam. After each of his visits Sam was restless. He would grumble to his family and friends about how bored he was, and how he never got a chance to try anything new and he was wasted stuck here at Pavilion Road day in day out. He would stare out of the windows. "Out there," he would say, "a mouse could breathe."

His wife, who had heard all this before, would snap, "Don't be silly, dear. You'd get lost in two minutes. Or the cat would have you. All very well for that pigeon, he's born to it." Sam's children would egg him on. "Go on, Dad," they would say, "dare you! Go out there!" And Sam would slip under the back door and saunter around for a while on the back doorstep, or even get as far as the edge of the back lawn, before he lost his nerve and came bolting back; "Got something in my eye," he would say, "Couldn't see where I was going any more . . ." or "Starting to rain. Better leave it till tomorrow."

For Sam was not quite the bold fellow he made himself out to be. Truth to tell the outside world scared him stiff — though it also fascinated him. He really did want to go out there and explore; but at the same time he was terrified of the idea. This mixture of feelings boiled away within him in the most uncomfortable way. He would force himself to venture out and then a noise or a shadow would set his heart thumping and he would scuttle back, furious with himself.

But one night he discovered the garage. The Dixons'

garage was close up beside the house and the first time Sam went in there he did so by mistake. He had not meant to go further than a few feet from the front door (he had wriggled through a gap in the draught excluder). He was scrounging inside a Mars bar wrapper dropped by one of the children when a sudden rustle sent him into a panic and he shot under the door of the garage, imagining every cat in the street on his tail.

Inside there was an enormous shiny monster, but Sam could see at once that it was dead so he paid it no attention and lurked cautiously by the wall until he was sure there were no further dangers. As well as the Dixons' car there was the lawnmower, a clutter of pots of paint and garden tools, and another, smaller and equally dead monster which was in fact a Honda motorbike. The Honda belonged to the Dixons' next door neighbour's son, Kevin, who was eighteen and worked at a factory a few miles away. Kevin used the motorbike to go to and from work, as well as to meet his friends in the evenings, and the Dixons allowed him to keep it in their garage. The Honda was Kevin's pride and joy: it sat there gleaming in the darkness, a blaze of silver and shiny black. Sam stared at it.

He crept across the oily floor, feeling very brave, and sniffed around it. Clearly, it was quite harmless. It smelled of petrol and polish but there was also another, more interesting smell coming from somewhere up above him. The smell of bacon-flavoured crisps. Now, if there was one thing Sam would go to any lengths to get, it was a bacon-flavoured crisp. He forgot all about cats and scary noises, swarmed up the side of the monster — with some difficulty since it was slippery — and sat on the saddle, sniffing frantically. Ah! The smell was coming from that deep white box behind. Sam peered over the edge — and there in the bottom was a bacon-flavoured crisp packet with at least three crisps

still in it. Joy of joys! Sam slithered down into the box and started to tuck in.

Next door, Kevin was coming downstairs, yawning dreadfully and trying not to wake his parents. It was five o'clock in the morning and he was on the early shift. He let himself out of the house, put on his crash helmet, yawned some more, and rolled up the Dixons' garage door.

Sam, in the bottom of the bike carrier, eating the best bacon-flavoured crisp of his life, heard the most appalling roaring sound and froze in horror. He crept under the crisp packet and kept quite still. Heavy footsteps approached. Two more packets of crisps and a foil-wrapped ham sandwich dropped down on top of him — Kevin's breakfast. The lid was slammed on the box, which began to rock violently from side to side. Sam, within, was flung to and fro; he squeaked in terror and scrabbled at the sides of the box. Too late, much too late.

Kevin wheeled the Honda out into the road, got on and kicked the starter.

There was the most deafening noise Sam had ever heard in his life. He juddered all over from nose to tail. And then the noise settled to a steady drone and the box jiggled and shook and bounced and Sam jiggled and shook and bounced with it. It was appalling. He had never been so scared in his life. It was worse by far than the teapot adventure. He had no idea what was happening. Was he in some kind of machine?

He knew about machines because of the fridge that hummed and buzzed in the Dixons' kitchen, and Mrs. Dixon's vacuum-cleaner that roared over his head when he was trying to sleep under the floorboards. But this machine, if that was what it was, seemed to have gone mad; it howled and growled and bounced — it appeared to be flying. Sam remembered all the times he had wished he could fly like the racing pigeon or the starlings. He moaned. If this was flying, he'd had enough. More than enough. And he never wanted to see another bacon-flavoured crisp in his life. Never ever. He was rolling around in bacon-flavoured crisps, down in the bottom of his thundering white prison; he stank of bacon-flavoured crisp; there were bits of bacon-flavoured crisp in his ears and clinging to his fur.

And then all of a sudden there was silence. The box ceased to bounce around; the dreadful roaring stopped.

Kevin switched off the Honda's engine and wheeled it to a place in the factory bike park. He was still yawning; the ten-minute run to work was something he did more or less in his sleep, when he was on the early shift. He opened the bike carrier, picked up his sandwich and his packets of crisps; he just missed picking up the end of Sam's tail too. He looked at his watch and saw that he was late, shoved the lid back without closing it properly, and rushed off.

Sam lay among bacon-flavoured crisps, gasping. He felt bruised and battered all over. He stretched his legs, gingerly; nothing seemed to be broken. He looked up and saw a crack of daylight. He tried to climb the side of the box, slipped back, jumped, slipped again, jumped once more and grabbed the edge of the box with his front paws. He hauled himself up and slithered through the crack and down the outside of the box without even looking to see where he was. All he wanted was to escape from this mad flying monster.

There was a great open space, far too much of it. Sam did not like open spaces. He scurried into a clump of grass and peered out.

The bike park was a patch of waste ground some distance from the factory. It was a scruffy place with black cindery earth, withered grass, a few bushes and much litter by way of tins and bottles and rotting newspapers. Nearby was a high wire fence and on the other side of the fence was the factory's rubbish tip. Sam, of course, did not know all this; he looked out of his sparse shelter, saw the row of sparkling motor-bikes, a Coke tin and a flapping copy of *The Sun* and thought this was the most horrible place on earth. He could feel wide high sky above him, which was terrifying, and could smell horrid and unfamiliar smells: smoke, exhaust fumes and disagreeable rubbish. He was too miserable to do anything but sit there, quivering.

All of a sudden he felt a great shadow come swooping down above him. Even a mouse that has led a sheltered life in a house has instincts about swooping shadows. Sam shot sideways out of the clump of grass and under a rusty petrol can. The great yellow beak of the seagull missed him by inches; the bird flapped away, squawking angrily. Sam, almost fainting, crouched under the petrol tin.

"You want to watch out for them," said a voice. "Nasty beggars. Not that they bother me a lot — they know I'll give as good as I get."

A large whiskered face was staring at him through the fence. Sam had never seen a rat before; Pavilion Road had many inhabitants but they did not include rats.

"Stopping here long?" enquired the rat. "There's good pickings, I can tell you." Sam shuddered. He looked beyond the rat towards the rubbish tip, which was a smoking waste-land that stank of decay. For a mouse accustomed to the best toast crumbs, it was a hideous prospect. Moreover, there was a seething mass of seagulls above it. A crow sat on a nearby post. Sam felt overcome with despair. He closed his eyes and gave a low moan.

"You look a bit off colour, mate," said the rat cheerfully. "Here, have a bit of this — it'll perk you up."

Sam opened his eyes and found a large chunk of mouldy raw bacon under his nose. It made him feel even worse, if possible. But it was kindly meant, evidently this rat was a decent enough fellow, and it wouldn't do to offend him. Sam pulled himself together and explained that he wasn't hungry, and that he was here by accident and wanted only to get away again. Though, he added hastily, he was sure it was a fine place if you were used to it.

"How come you're here anyway?" enquired the rat.

"I flew," said Sam, shuddering at the memory.

"Stupid . . . That's for birds." The rat began to eat the mouldy bacon. "Anyway, while you're here you want to have a look round. Best tip in town, this is. Rotten potatoes, mattresses, old TV sets — you name it, we've got it. The other day a bloke brought a whole load of burnt chips. Wow! Did we have a blow-out!"

Sam came out from under the petrol can, with a cautious glance skywards.

'Come on," said the rat, "I'll give you a tour of the best stuff."

Sam followed him through the wire fence and out into a world of hills and valleys and sudden terrible craters, a world that flapped and stank, that even smoked in places. There were great heaps of old clothes and heaving plastic, valleys of ash and cinders, horrid holes filled with smelly oily water. There were fridges without doors and rusty cookers, old shoes and prams and lawn mowers. The rat had his home in an upside-down sofa, a fine mansion of springs and foam rubber, most impressive. It smelled, though, of mould, damp and bad fish. The rat was not a fussy house-keeper. Sam's whiskers twitched as he picked his way among fish-bones and other leavings. He thought of Pavilion Road with its clean floors and smells of polish, soap and toast. Tears came into his eyes.

"Sit down," said the rat. "Make yourself at home."

And then from somewhere above and beyond there came a tremendous grinding and whooshing noise. The rat leapt up.

"Oops!" he cried. "Fresh supplies! Let's get going!"

Sam hurried after him out into the rubbish tip again; it seemed better to stick to the only friend he had in this awful place. He was just in time to see a monstrous yellow machine fling a shower of rubbish on top of all that was already there. Immediately the sky was full of seagulls, squawking and squabbling; Sam, cowering under a plastic bag, could see glaring yellow eyes, snapping bills and great claws. The rat, apparently unworried, dashed out, dug around and returned with a banana skin. Had Sam come upon this at Pavilion Road he would have considered it quite a find, but as it was all he could do was mutter again that he wasn't hungry. The rat munched the banana skin and looked thoughtfully at Sam. "You're a funny bloke . . . You don't eat. You jump out of your skin every two seconds. What's wrong?"

"I want to go home," said Sam dolefully.

The rat finished the banana skin and started on a cabbage leaf. "*How* did you say you got here?"

Sam explained. Rather more precisely this time: the fearful shiny machine that roared and flew; the white box.

"Oh!" exclaimed the rat. "One of *those* . . . I'm with you now. Well, you'll have to go back the same way, won't you?"

He plunged off into the tip once more, past bicycle wheels and old tyres and mounds of detergent bottles, with Sam panting behind. When they got to the wire fence again the rat waved a paw. "There you are," he said, "which one?"

Sam looked. There, not far away, was a whole row of shiny machines — dozens of them, all of them, so far as he could see, exactly alike. Most of them had a white box at the back. The flicker of hope that he had felt died down. He looked hopelessly at the rat.

"Why did you get in there in the first place?" asked the rat, with a touch of impatience.

"Bacon-flavoured crisps!" cried Sam, inspired. "That's it! It'll be the one that smells of bacon-flavoured crisps. That was why I got into the box."

"Ah!" said the rat. "Now you're talking. Let's get going, then."

He scuttled over to the machines and began to sniff his way along the row. Chip butties . . . chicken leg . . . Mars Bar . . . Ah! What about this, then?"

And as he spoke he swarmed up the back wheel of one of the machines. From the seat he peered down at Sam. "Are you getting any sort of bacon-flavoured crisp pong down there?"

"Yes, I am!" cried Sam excitedly.

"Come on up," instructed the rat.

Sam scrambled up. And they both saw, now, that the lid of the white box was slightly open. And from within there came, indeed, a fine and reassuring smell of bacon-flavoured crisp.

"Well," said the rat, "you're in luck. Cheerio, then."

Sam said good-bye warmly and thanked him for his trouble. The rat vanished and Sam slithered down inside the white box and crept underneath the empty crisp packet. He was trembling now at the thought of another of those dreadful journeys. His ordeal was by no means over. But by now he was exhausted. He closed his eyes, sighed, and fell fast asleep.

He woke with a start to find the box shuddering and the machine roaring. At first he thought he was in a nightmare and then it all came back. He clung onto the crisp packet and settled down, grimly, to wait for it to be over. Which, after a hideous interval, it was. The machine ceased to fly, the roaring became a grumble and ceased altogether. Sam braced himself; he knew what he had to do if he was to escape.

The lid of the box was lifted and at the same moment Sam leapt out. Kevin gave a yelp of surprise as Sam dashed up his sleeve, sprang on to the garage floor and shot behind some old sacks. For the next couple of days Kevin would be telling anyone who would listen a tale about how a mouse had jumped out of his bike carrier, which of course no one believed.

Sam waited until he had gone, and then crept out and back into Fifty-four Pavilion Road. He slipped into a familiar back alley that ran behind the kitchen wainscot to his home under the stairs, where his family were having a mid-day snooze.

"There you are, dear," said his wife, "we were just wondering. Where've you been, then?"

Sam took a deep breath. And then he began to talk of machines that flew, of birds the size of cushions, of a place that reached further than you could see in every direction and in which there were sights and smells that were beyond description. He grew big and bold

again as he talked. He told them of his friend the rat. He was Sam the traveller, Sam the intrepid, Sam the glorious.

And his family, who had heard this kind of thing before, listened up to a point. The children whispered and fidgetted. Their mother dozed. Once, the youngest child nudged her and said, "Ma — is Father telling the truth?" at which she woke up and said sternly, "Your father *always* tells the truth," — then dozed off again.

Chapter Six

NAT AND THE SPIDER BATTLE

Nat, the wood-louse, was not quite like other wood-lice. He looked exactly like them: stiff armour-plated back, fourteen legs, small black eyes, long whiskers. Even his own mother couldn't tell him apart from the rest of her children. But he had a mind of his own, a spirit of independence — you will remember the great bath climb — and he liked to keep himself to himself. He visited, from time to time, places that other wood-lice prefer to avoid — the bedroom windowsill, the kitchen floor.

It was thus — prowling around under the kitchen table one day — that disaster befell him. Mrs. Dixon happened to be sweeping up. Nat, trundling along without a thought in his head, found himself attacked from above by some immense descending cloud, hurled along the floor and tumbled with dust, crumbs and bits of paper into a red cavern (the dustpan) and thence into a fearful, smelly pit (the waste-bin).

He unrolled himself (wood-lice, like hedgehogs, curl up when alarmed). He sighed. Well, he thought, I'll have to get meself out of here, won't I? He began to forge his way upwards through potato peelings, lettuce leaves and newspaper. After what seemed a long time he saw daylight. He ploughed onwards and came out at last through a crack onto a shiny top. This had a nasty slippery feel so he set off once more, up a wooden cliff that was quite an easy climb. This was in fact the side of the sink unit and when Nat **reached the top he** found himself on a shining silver plain with ridges along which he slithered uncomfortably. Don't like this place, he thought, I'll have to get away from here . . . And no sooner had he thought it than his legs slid from under him altogether and he found himself tumbling over the edge and down, down, down . . .

And splash into the washing-up bowl, which was half filled with water.

Now I've gone and done it, thought Nat. He floated on his back, his fourteen legs kicking hopelessly. He floated round and round in circles. Well, he thought, I don't see how I'm going to get out of this one. He floated in glum resignation, staring up at the distant ceiling, which he couldn't even see. So that's that, he thought.

"Having fun?"

Nat swivelled one eye, in so far as this was possible. There on the edge of the washing-up bowl was perched the spider. His friend the spider.

"No," said Nat, "since you ask."

"I thought you people couldn't swim?"

"We can't," said Nat, "that's the problem."

"Ah," said the spider, "why didn't you say so? Watch out!" And so saying, he began to shoot out a silken line which spun slowly towards Nat. "Grab hold," instructed the spider. "And hang on tight."

Nat seized the thread with as many legs as he could and clung on. He felt himself dragged across the water and then swung upwards.

The spider had vanished. "Thanks," cried Nat breathlessly, "That'll do nicely. Thanks a lot . . ." But still he went spinning upwards, clinging onto the spider's silk rope, upwards and upwards, dizzyingly, the sink unit and the washing-up bowl now distant beneath him. And there was the spider again, he saw, scuttling up the window-frame at enormous speed, pausing once to let out more thread, then dashing on up.

"Hey," called Nat, whirling round and round, going up and up. "Hey . . . That's enough."

But on he went, and on went the spider, vanishing again now into a crack at the corner of the window, and on went Nat until suddenly he too reached the crack, found his feet on solid ground once more and the spider grinning out at him. Help! thought Nat, *Now* where am I?"

"This is my pad," said the spider, "Care for some fly?"

"No, thanks," said Nat. "I'm a vegetarian."

"Suit yourself. Excuse me a minute — small repair job I should see to."

They were high up at the top of the kitchen window. Far down below were the sink and the table and the fridge and the cooker. And Willie the dog, asleep on the mat beside the boiler. The spider's web, Nat now saw, was stretched right across one corner of the window, a fine and intricate affair like a great wheel of spokes and cross-bars. There was another, smaller one the other side. The spider was bustling around some broken lines. He came back, grumbling. "Bluebottles. Get one of those darn things thrashing around and there's a night's work gone west. Well, how d'you like it up here?"

"Very nice," said Nat politely. "Fine view." He was thinking what a long time it was going to take to crawl down again and find his way back to the nest in the back of the china cupboard, where his family was living at the moment.

"It's all mine," said the spider, "As far as you can see. My territory." He waved a leg around. "The window is mine and the ceiling as far as the light fitting and behind the freezer is mine and the top shelf of the dresser."

"I see," said Nat. After a moment he added, "Whose is the rest?"

The spider growled. He gnashed his teeth, up to a point and in so far as spiders have teeth. He really was a ferocious-looking fellow. "My neighbour's," he snarled.

Nat thought. He looked at the spider's legs, two of which were still somewhat shorter than the rest. "Is that the one you had the argument with," he enquired, "that you told me about last time?"

"That's him," snapped the spider.

"Ah," said Nat. Spiders must be a funny lot, he thought. What was all this about territories, and chopping each other's legs off? Wood-lice, it should be said, are peaceable creatures who browse quietly in flocks with seldom a cross word, except for some rather stern discipline of the young. I dunno, thought Nat . . . Still, they say it takes all sorts to make a world.

All of a sudden the spider appeared to go crazy. He hunched himself into a black baleful knot, which somehow made him look even more fierce than before; he blew himself out until he seemed twice as large as he really was; he huffed and puffed, he growled and gnashed.

"What's the matter?" asked Nat nervously.

"There he is!" spat the spider.

Nat looked. And there on the far side of the window, he saw, was another spider. Also hunching itself and blowing itself out, glaring and snarling.

"All right . . ." roared the spider. "If that's the way you want it . . . Here I come!"

Bless my soul, thought Nat, what a fuss . . . The spider went galloping off across the top of the window; the other spider advanced from his corner. And in the middle they met, with a horrid sound (to Nat) of clashing legs, shouts and oaths. The two spiders clutched each other round the middle like Japanese wrestlers; they swiped at each other with their back ends. Nat's friend succeeded in shoving his rival off the window altogether, but he merely dropped down a foot or so on a length of thread and then came swarming up again, back to the fray. They rampaged to and fro. The noise (to Nat) was quite terrible. It seemed extraordinary that, far below, the dog Willie should be sleeping in front of the boiler and Mrs. Dixon having a cup of coffee without paying the slightest attention.

"Take that!" panted Nat's friend . . . And, "Gotcha!" roared his neighbour.

Oh dear, thought Nat, there goes another leg! And indeed both spiders were beginning to look somewhat the worse for wear. Nat's friend was down to six legs again; the enemy had lost the whole of one and half of another two. And then all of a sudden they stopped, backed off, and the battle was apparently over.

The spider returned, out of breath. "There!" he said.

"How did you like that? Good, wasn't it!"

"Who won?" enquired Nat.

"A draw," said the spider. "It always is. That way we start again level the next time."

"What was it about?"

"About?" The spider stared irritably at Nat. "What d'you mean — what was it about? It wasn't about anything."

"I mean," said Nat, "why do you fight him?"

The spider became even more irritable. "Because as soon as I see him I feel like fighting. In fact even talking about him makes me feel like fighting. Grr . . ." And he began to rattle his legs threateningly.

Nat thought it best to change the subject. "I'd better be pushing off. My folks will be wondering where I've got to."

"No need to rush," said the spider. "You haven't seen my larder."

Nat wasn't at all sure that he wanted to, but it seemed wisest to oblige so he followed the spider into his den, a crack in the window-frame leading to a hole in the wall. There, neat parcels done up in silk thread were stacked in rows. The spider contemplated them, a little gloomily. "Mind, you can get tired of fly, day in day out. Sometimes I wonder about experimenting a bit."

Nat backed away quickly. "I wouldn't do that," he said, "my mum always says you shouldn't go against nature."

"I daresay not," said the spider. "All the same, life gets tedious. One builds webs. One fights. One eats fly. What's the point of it all, I sometimes wonder." He glared at Nat, as though it might be in some way his fault. "Don't you?"

"No," said Nat "I have enough trouble with falling on my back and not being able to get right way up again."

"You're the wrong shape," said the spider.

Nat began to say that that was a matter of opinion, and then thought better of it. "It's a good shape for some things," he observed.

"Such as?"

"Getting through cracks. Going under stones."

The spider sniffed. "Possibly."

"Of course," said Nat, "I can see it's another matter altogether being able to make webs and drop from enormous heights on a line."

"Right!" exclaimed the spider, brightening up.

"And fourteen legs is rather too many, whereas eight is just about right. Or six . . ." he added, with a quick glance at the spider.

"Exactly!"

"Still," said Nat with a sigh, "there it is. One makes the best of it. And now I really must be off."

"Shall I give you a hand?" enquired the spider graciously.

But Nat replied that no, it was very kind but he would make his own way home. And he set off on his slow journey down the wall, trundling along at his own speed, avoiding slippery places, looking for crumbly plaster and rough wood that his fourteen legs could get

a grip on. Here we go, he said to himself, steady does it, all the time in the world . . .

And as he went the life of the Dixon kitchen raged around him. The children came home from school and had their tea. Everyone talked at once. Someone spilled a bottle of milk. Mrs. Dixon stepped on Willie. Nobody at all was even aware of Nat, making his slow and patient journey from the top of the window to the bottom of the china cupboard, except the baby, who spotted him working his way down the dresser and pointed and said something to which no one paid any attention. Nat waved his whiskers at the baby and continued. And when at last he reached his nest, where all his friends and relations were curled up under damp plaster behind Mrs. Dixon's wedding-present vase that she never used, his mother said suspiciously, "Where've you been, then?"

"Nowhere," said Nat. And went to sleep.

Chapter Seven

WILLIE AND THE GREAT HOLE

Willie, the small square white terrier, loved two things in the world: food and Mrs. Dixon. He was never absolutely certain which he loved best. He admired and adored Mrs. Dixon and had thrilling dreams in which he protected her from armed robbers and the milkman and the television repair man and Mr. Dixon's brother Bob whom Willie hated and had once tried to bite. Food, though, was in a class of its own. Willie would eat absolutely anything, especially if it wasn't his. He was mostly obliged to eat tinned dogfood, but he was perfectly prepared to try anything at all, and in the past had bolted down a large lump of builders' putty, half a pound of chocolate fudge, a slab of uncooked frozen pastry and a letter from Mrs. Dixon's aunt with a cheque for ten pounds in it. Admittedly, some of this had been when he was much younger but even now — when he was probably middle-aged — no one knew — he was prepared to try anything. From time to time, he was allowed a bone, but Mrs. Dixon was not keen on this since he always tried to bury it in unsuitable places, such as behind the sofa cushions or under the front door mat.

On the morning in question Mrs. Dixon went out shopping. Since it was a fine warm day she left the back door open so that Willie could go out in the garden if he wanted. There was a belief in the Dixon family that Willie would protect the house from burglars.

Willie, once she had gone, howled for a minute or two in protest and then wandered around the kitchen in case anyone had left anything edible out where he could get it. No one had.

He sat down in the sun on the back doorstep, feeling bored and discontented. He looked down the garden; a blackbird was stalking worms on the lawn, a clutch of sparrows were squabbling — nothing worth taking any interest in. And then as he watched, the blackbird flew off with a shriek, the sparrows fled, and the cat from next door slipped over the wall and loped towards the apple tree.

Willie hurled himself after it, barking fit to burst. The cat slid up the trunk of the tree, sat on a branch and looked down at him.

"Idiot," it said. "You never learn, do you?"

Willie, breathless, glared up at it. The cat yawned, stretched out a leg and started on a tricky grooming job. "All on your own again?" it enquired. "Poor little fellow all on his ownsomes, is he?"

"Oh, shut up!" snarled Willie "One of these days I'll get you, just you wait, one of these days I'll . . ."

"Don't make me laugh," said the cat.

Willie, fuming, sat down to get his breath back.

"I know what I'd do if I was you," said the cat. "I'd dig up that bone they've buried in the rose bed."

Now Willie was not stupid, but he was weak. He pricked up his ears; he looked at the cat suspiciously. A warning voice in his head said, "Never trust a cat;" another voice cried, "Bone! Bone! Bone!"

"What bone?" said Willie, at last.

"The bone they buried in the rose bed," said the cat

"The bone who buried?"

"Your people," said the cat, "the other day."

Willie looked towards the rose bed. He sniffed. Could there be — just ever so faintly — a whiff, the merest whiff, of bone? "They never bury bones in the rose bed," he said, after a few moments.

"There's always a first time," said the cat.

Willie got up and walked over to the rose bed. He

looked at it. Roses. Other little green leafy things with flowers on them. Earth. Freshly dug earth. Smells of . . . flowers and earth and . . . and *could* there just be something else?

"Mutton bone," said the cat. "Leg, I'd have said."

Willie began to dig. Cautiously. Then a little harder. Earth flew. One of the green leafy things with a flower fell to pieces. Then another. Willie paused and snuffed.

Was that a hint — just a hint — of mutton bone?

"A long way down, it was," continued the voice from the apple tree. "Great big leg of lamb. Nice and meaty."

Willie dug. He dug and dug. Earth flew in all directions, along with flowers and leaves and the roots of roses. The hole grew larger and larger. It was a pit, now, and Willie was right inside it, digging furiously. He was no longer a small square white terrier but a small square brown terrier. His feet were caked with mud and his fur was coated with it. He was enjoying himself; digging is what terriers do best. Willie had frequently been scolded for digging so well in places that Mrs. Dixon did not want dug. Such as rose beds. But right now Willie had clean forgotten about that. He was digging the deepest hole he had ever dug in his life and somewhere at the bottom of it there was going to be the most enormous Bone.

Eventually he had to stop because he was getting worn out. He sat back, panting. There was no rose bed any more, just this enormous hole. Nor was there any bone. Willie climbed out of his hole and looked at it doubtfully. He couldn't smell bone at all any more, not even the faintest whiff. And the more he looked at the hole the more it gave him the most uncomfortable feeling. He didn't think Mrs. Dixon was going to think it was a very nice hole.

Willie looked round for the cat. It was no longer there.

But the hole was. Very much there. Large, deep and muddy. There seemed to be more hole than garden, indeed.

Willie was no longer feeling energetic and happy and he had lost all interest in bones. He stared miserably at the hole. He could think of no way in which to undig a hole. Whatever was he to do?

The only thing was to hope that Mrs. Dixon might think someone else had dug it. He cheered up. He would get himself nice and clean and be fast asleep in his basket when Mrs. Dixon came back. "Hole?" he would say, "What hole?" He went inside and rolled briskly all over the sitting room carpet. Lots of mud came off. He got on the sofa and rolled on that too; more mud came off. Willie was pleased — he was a great deal cleaner now. He still didn't feel quite right, though, so he went into the kitchen where he spotted a pile of clothes that Mrs. Dixon had just ironed laid out on a chair. They looked like just the thing for cleaning yourself up with, so he pulled them off and rolled on them vigorously for several minutes. At the end of this Willie was really quite clean. He shook himself, had a drink of water to cool himself down, and got into his basket to wait for Mrs. Dixon to come back. He was tired. Presently he dozed off.

"Wotcha!"

Willie woke up with a start. Sam, the mouse, was sitting on the edge of the dresser, looking down at him.

"Be quiet," said Willie. "I'm asleep." He closed his eyes again.

"Pity." Sam began cleaning his whiskers one by one. "I had a rather amusing idea. What would you say to a nice juicy bone?"

Willie opened his eyes. He licked his lips. The hole, the cat, the mud were all forgotten. "Bone? Where's there a bone?"

"In there." Sam waved a paw in the direction of the waste-bin.

Willie knew all about the waste-bin. It was three feet tall, made of brown plastic and had a tightly fitting lid. It smelled delicious, always, but Mrs. Dixon never forgot to put the lid back on. It was on right now. He looked sourly at Sam. "So?"

"So a smart dog could jump up at it until he knocked it over. Lid comes off. Bone falls out. So do bread crumbs and broken biscuits and nice things like that," added Sam.

Willie thought about this. "You think?"

"Try it and see."

Willie got out of his basket. He eyed the dustbin. He sniffed. Bone? Definitely bone, now he came to think about it.

He flung himself at the dustbin. He scrabbled with his paws. The dustbin rocked slightly. Willie flung himself again, scrabbling more. Eggshells, cabbage leaves, empty tins and potato peelings tumbled out all over the kitchen floor. Sam shinned down the side of the dresser and got busy.

"Good work," he said, his mouth full of ryvita. "Spot on."

"Where's the bone?" said Willie, eyeing the mess. He couldn't see any bone. Come to that he couldn't even smell bone any more.

Willie nosed around. He ate a tea-bag, which didn't taste very nice, and spat it out again. There was no bone anywhere. Just a great deal of mess which was now giving him the same sort of uncomfortable feeling that the hole had. He began to think of Mrs. Dixon again. Sam was still gorging himself on crumbs. Willie started to tell Sam that this hadn't been such an amusing idea after all when he heard the front door open.

Sam vanished between a crack in the floor boards. Willie looked round the kitchen. There were muddy shirts spread all over the rug and a trail of rubbish from the dustbin.

Willie got back into his basket and tried to look like a dog that has been asleep for a long, long time.

Mrs. Dixon was carrying the baby and a basket of shopping. She took one look at the kitchen and shrieked. She didn't even see Willie. She put the baby in the playpen and the shopping on the table. Willie shot under a chair. Mrs. Dixon went into the sitting

66

room, saw the muddy carpet and the muddy sofa and shrieked again. Willie cowered, his tail between his legs. Mrs. Dixon said, "WILLIE!" He heard her go out of the back door into the garden. He heard her bawl, "WILLIE . . .!"

Then she came back into the kitchen.

No, Mrs. Dixon didn't beat Willie. Could you beat a small square terrier that is lying on its back with all four paws in the air and its tail between its legs? She said a lot, though. So did Willie. Willie said, "It wasn't my fault, honest, it was that cat and that mouse and I never meant to and I think you're wonderful and I'll lick your feet if you want me to and I don't like bones that much anyway." But of course Mrs. Dixon didn't understand a word of this.

Chapter Eight

SAM AND THE
MOUSE MANSION

In spring Fifty-four Pavilion Road became even more crowded than it already was. It already sheltered five humans, thirty-nine animals and several thousand insects. As soon as April arrived the birds moved in also. The gutters were taken over by sparrows, squabbling for the best nest sites; the jackdaws arrived and started to drop sticks down the chimney, also with nesting in mind. The sticks would land in the fireplace from which Mrs. Dixon would remove them, grumbling. The next day the jackdaws would patiently drop more down and Mrs. Dixon, less patiently, would remove them again.

All this had an effect on others, also. It made Sam's wife restless. We have not, so far, heard much of Sam's wife. She was called Doris and was a mouse who did not always assert herself but could be extremely obstinate if she wished. This mouse family, you remember, lived in the cupboard under the stairs. "I want a new nest," said Doris, one April morning.

"Nonsense," retorted Sam, "we're fine where we are."

"No we're not," snapped Doris, with a look in her eye that Sam knew well. His heart sank.

"We've always lived here. And our parents before us and their parents before that and . . ."

"So?" said Doris coldly.

"We're used to it."

"You make me sick," said Doris.

The children were busy giving Sam warning nudges. When their mother was in this mood, they well knew, there was no point in arguing. Sam, though, crashed on, pointing out that their present home was convenient and full of things he was fond of such as pieces of bacon rind that were now valuable antiques and layers of shredded newspaper that he liked to read in his spare time. "I've got bits of the Daily Mirror going back to 1967. It's a priceless collection. I can't just walk out on it. And where'd I be without the gym? How'd I do my work-outs?" Sam's gym was an old wire desk-tray that Mr. Dixon had once pushed away at the back of the stair cupboard and which Sam now used for gymnastic exercises, swinging hand over hand around it and generally showing off.

"I!" cried Doris. "I, I, I! I this, I that, I the other thing! And what about me? Do I have to spend the rest of my life in a seedy run-down dump? Do I have to do without up-to-date furnishings and modern conveniences just because of you?" She became shrill with passion. "Do I have to fester in a slum to satisfy you? And what about my babies?"

"We're fine, Mum," said the children hastily. "Honest. Absolutely fine."

"I don't mean you," said Doris, "I mean the new babies." And she flounced out without another word.

Sam groaned.

He was the father of — at a rough guess — twenty-nine already. A few of these had come to nothing on account of unfortunate accidents of one kind or another; most had left the nest and set up on their own. Some had even left Fifty-four Pavilion Road and moved next door, having married into other families. The last lot — some half dozen or so — were still living with their parents under the stairs, along with various sisters and cousins who were part of the family. Sam was a reasonably good father and perfectly well aware that he was just as responsible for a new crop of children as was his wife. Even so, he groaned. Fortunately Doris was by now out of earshot.

She was on her way upstairs to the Dixon children's playroom. This was a place that, normally, the mice avoided. There was not much to be had by way of pickings except the odd abandoned toffee or crisp packet with crumbs, and it was full of things that did not interest them by way of paint-boxes and toy trains and Lego bricks. But right now there was something that interested Doris very much. The Dixons had just gone on holiday. The house was wonderfully quiet and peaceful. The mice could come and go as they liked, day and night, bold as brass, and Doris, wandering around and grumbling to herself about the shortcomings of her home, had discovered something fascinating.

It had been given to Andy Dixon for his birthday just before the family went off for their holiday. There it stood, on a shelf in the corner of the playroom, and Doris had taken one look and fallen in love — in so far as it is possible to fall in love with a toy garage. It was painted crisply white and it had a red roof and green double doors. It was in fact only half of the birthday present — the other half was the car that lived inside it and which Andy had taken away on holiday with him which was why the garage stood there empty. Doris had already discovered that if she pushed at the doors with her nose they would open and once inside . . . well, once inside she knew that this was the perfect nesting place for which she had always been searching.

She set to work.

Some hours later the children reported to Sam, who was having a snooze on the sitting room sofa. With the Dixons — and Willie — away such risks could be taken.

70

"Ma's nesting," they reported.

Sam opened one eye. "Whassat?"

"Ma's nesting. Come and see."

They led Sam up to the playroom, not by the usual secret by-ways in walls and under floors but boldly up the front stairs. They led him to the garage, from within which came faint scuffling sounds.

"You there, dear?" enquired Sam, cautiously.

There was no reply. Then the door opened a crack, Doris put her nose out and said sharply, "What do you want? I'm busy."

She was indeed. There was a glimpse of wonders within. To be precise, a magnificent upholstery of shredded pink knitting wool, taken from Mrs. Dixon's work-basket, a lining of lilac-coloured kleenex, minced into tiny scraps by sharp teeth.

"You can look," said Doris, holding the door open a crack. "Don't anybody touch."

Sam and the children surveyed the nest.

"Pretty, isn't it?" said Doris graciously. "The pink's nice with the lilac, don't you think?"

Sam swallowed. "Lovely, dear. Very nice."

"Bye, then," said Doris, starting to close the door.

"Hang on . . ." said Sam. "What about me and the children, then?"

"What about you?" enquired Doris, staring. "You're stopping under the stairs, aren't you? You like it there."

"You can't leave me to manage that lot all on my own!" wailed Sam.

Doris smiled sweetly. "Why not? You'll be good, won't you?" she added, to the children.

"Yes, Mum," said the children, smirking horribly.

Doris closed the garage door. There came further sounds of busy scuffling and bustling from within.

I hesitate to tell you what followed. The mouse children ran wild. Their behaviour went from bad to

worse. They had always been reasonably good
children; Sam used to bawl them out from time to time
when they were being a nuisance but by and large he
didn't pay much attention to them. Now that he had to
cope with them himself life became simply terrible The
children rampaged all over the house; they risked their
lives scooting round the lavatory seat, they played
parachute off the curtains, they wriggled into the
marmalade pot and came out all sticky, they whooped
it up from dusk till dawn and dawn till dusk. Each time

Sam tried to count them there were two or three missing. He wasn't even entirely sure how many there ought to be and when he asked them they said they didn't know either. Grey from worry and lack of sleep, Sam hunted his children from the kitchen to the sitting room and up the stairs to the bathroom and even up in the loft.

After several days he could stand it no longer. He went up to the playroom and tapped humbly at the garage door. A muffled voice told him to go away.

"Please come home," Sam implored his wife. "They're driving me barmy."

Doris put her nose out. She was looking comfortable, rather sleepy and distinctly fat. "No, thank you," she said, "I'm nicely set up here." And indeed Sam, peering into the garage, could see further marvels of decoration; there was now a picture of the Queen propped up in one corner (a First Class stamp) and some elegant cushions of pale yellow cotton wool strewn around.

Sam took a deep breath. "Tell you what," he said, "I'll do the old place up for you."

"I bet," said Doris. "I'll believe that when I see it."

"I swear," said Sam. "You see . . ." And all of a sudden it came to him that this would be his greatest and grandest achievement. She would see all right. Was he not Sam the Great? Had he not escaped from a tea-pot and travelled to the ends of the earth on a fearful machine? Oh, she would indeed see. He would create a nest such as had never been seen before.

He whisked downstairs and set to work.

The family home in the cupboard under the stairs was in fact a cardboard shoebox, filled with layers of newspaper, scraps of this and that and general rubbish amid which they had been living for years. Sam lined the children up. "Clear it out," he ordered, "Everything out! The lot! Then report to me for further instructions." The children, impressed by his air of passion and determination, stopped fooling around and set to.

Sam also got to work. He scurried from one end of Fifty-four Pavilion Road to the other. Not for nothing had he spent every night of his life roaming and exploring; he knew every cupboard and every corner, he knew what was where. He knew, now, where to find everything he needed. He sent the children up to the loft, into the dustbins and the beds, he had them panting to and fro, tugging and pulling and heaving. And as they realised what their father was intent upon, as the grandeur of the scheme dawned upon them, as they realised what it was they were constructing, they entered into the spirit of it. "Cor, Dad!" they exclaimed. "Smashing! This is going to be great! Ace! Spot on!"

The shoe-box was to become a palace.

First of all it was carpeted with chunks of foam rubber nibbled from an old mattress in the loft. In the centre was placed a magnificent rug of red wool (one of Andy Dixon's winter gloves). The walls were papered in gold and silver with Christmas wrapping paper. At this point Sam got quite carried away with the daring of his design and added a gold foil angel from the Christmas tree decoration box. This was to stand in one corner with tinsel around its neck. "That's a sculpture," he instructed the children. "You only get those in very high-class homes." The children gazed in awe, and then rushed off on further errands.

The beds were made from layer upon layer of shredded scarlet tissue paper. And the central point of Sam's grand design was now revealed. A knitting-needle, hauled from Mrs. Dixon's work-basket, was stuck across the top of the shoe-box; a lace handkerchief, draped over it, formed a curtain. There were now two rooms.

It was at this point that the youngest child came panting down from upstairs with news.

"Dad, I got something to tell you. Ma's had babies."

Sam, intent upon arranging the folds of the lace handkerchief to best advantage, paused. "Ah," he said. "How many?" he added, after a moment.

"I dunno," said the child. "Lots, anyway."

"Never mind," said Sam robustly. He sat down and considered. And then he had a further idea. He summoned half a dozen of the largest and strongest of the children.

The cradle was a large match-box, lined with feathers from the Dixons' pillows. This was set up in one corner and Sam set about the final touches. "The best homes," he informed the children, "have Art. This home is going to have Art on the walls." And he produced a cheese advertisement in full colour taken from one of Mrs. Dixon's magazines, showing a mouth-watering slice of cheddar. "That is a Still Life," said Sam, arranging it against the Christmas wrapping paper, "and this . . ." — here he produced a passport photo of Mr. Dixon that he had found in the desk — ". . . is a family portrait." And, as a last-minute inspiration, he raided the kitchen cupboard and fetched two bright blue birthday cake candle-holders complete with pink candles which were set up on either side of the entrance to the shoe-box and delighted the children more than anything.

"And now we're ready," said Sam. "Go and tell your mother."

The children hurried upstairs. "Ma!" they cried, "Dad's made a new nest."

Doris looked at them suspiciously. "No, he never," he said.

"Yes, he has!" they cried.

"Not your dad."

"Honest, Ma! Come and see!"

At last they persuaded her. She tucked her new
babies (there were in fact eight of them, each about half
an inch long, pink and hairless) up on a cotton wool
cushion and followed the children down to the stair
cupboard, where Sam was sitting proudly outside his
mansion.

"Hello, dear," he said.

Doris was speechless. She gazed incredulously at
the pink candles in the blue holders and then she
entered the shoe-box and inspected it, slowly, and in
silence. Everyone held their breath and waited. Then
she came out again.

"Like it?" said Sam.

76

There was a silence. "It'll do," said Doris.

And that was how Doris came home again. The babies were brought down from the garage and arranged in the matchbox lined with feathers (Sam did a quick count and groaned slightly — he was now the father of around forty-three). Doris fetched the First Class stamp and put it up beside the passport photo of Mr. Dixon. And everybody settled down in the refurbished home — or at least in so far as a family of around eighteen can be said to settle down.

And the Dixons, when they returned from their holiday, were much puzzled about several things; such as why Andy's garage was full of kleenex and knitting wool, why two of the birthday cake candle-holders had vanished and why there were shreds of Christmas wrapping paper all over the house.

Chapter Nine

THE SPIDER
AND THE PEARL

Mrs. Dixon was squeamish about spiders. She waged war upon them with dusters and dustpan. It has to be said, though, that the feeling was mutual. The spider who lived above the kitchen window — a fierce fellow who had won many a famous battle — used to say that the very sight of Mrs. Dixon made him feel quite faint. "It's the colour," he declared. "That ghastly yellowish pink. And the size of her. Ugh!"

This particular spider was very proud of his home, in which, he claimed, his parents and grandparents had lived before him. His friend Nat, the young wood-louse, visited him there from time to time and listened with resignation while the spider held forth about his fine view ("On a clear day I can see right through the kitchen door and out into the hall") and his amazing collection of antique fly wings ("This is a rare specimen caught by my great-uncle"); the spider was somewhat boring about all this. Also, he was inclined to brag.

One day, however, Nat found him in distinctly low spirits. He did not seem to be himself at all. He was sitting outside his home in a state of dejection; his web was tattered in several places and he was making no attempt to repair it.

"Hello!" said Nat cheerfully.

The spider grunted and twiched a leg in response.

"Anything wrong?" enquired Nat.

The spider sighed. "I don't want to talk about it."

"Go on," said Nat, "You'll feel better."

"It's hopeless," groaned the spider. "There's no point. And it's humiliating. Me, of all people. That this should happen to me."

"*What*?" Nat was becoming a touch impatient.

"Her . . ." moaned the spider. "Her above the dresser." He waved a leg. "Gorgeous creature . . . Want her to marry me. Don't know how to set about it. May as well die."

"Gracious!" said Nat.

The truth emerged. Above the dresser lived a female spider with whom Nat's friend had fallen suddenly in love. He wished to persuade her to marry him and live in his home.

"Well," said Nat, "go ahead, then." He couldn't see the point, himself, but the spider was evidently in a bad way.

"You don't understand. She's choosy. You've got to set about it right. Presents. The right presents. Better than anyone else's presents."

"Who else?"

The spider spluttered. For a moment or two he was his old fighting self.

"Him! My neighbour. He's after her too. Aagh . . . Even thinking about it makes me want to fight him. Just let me get at him! I'll have his legs off . . . I'll, I'll . . ."

"All right," said Nat hastily, "so give her presents then. Sounds easy."

"D'you think I haven't tried?" The spider collapsed into gloom again. "I've tried fly. The very best fly — gift-wrapped. I've tried moth. I've tried ladybird. I've tried silverfish. She just looks down her nose at all of them. I've run out of things to try. Except . . ." He perked up for a moment and looked intently at Nat.

"No," said Nat, "definitely not. They don't like wood-lice. It's a well-known fact."

"Is that so?" The spider lost interest. He sighed deeply. He seemed close to tears.

"Maybe she doesn't want something to eat."

"Of course she wants something to eat. Everyone wants something to eat."

"Perhaps she wants something beautiful to look at?" suggested Nat.

The spider stared. "Whatever would she want that for?"

"Some do," said Nat. "It's a matter of taste."

The spider looked perplexed. "So where would I find something beautiful?" he asked, after a moment.

"Under the cooker," said Nat promptly.

"You're joking."

"No, I'm not." And Nat began to explain.

Some weeks ago Mrs. Dixon had broken her artificial pearl necklace. There had been a good deal of commotion at the time, with pearls scattered all over the kitchen floor and everyone down on their hands and knees collecting them. The pearls had been gathered up, or at least so the Dixons thought, and indeed the necklace was now around Mrs. Dixon's neck again. But one pearl had rolled under the cooker, and there it had lain ever since. Nat, trundling around, had come across it several times and had admired it. Indeed he had thought of giving it to his mother for her birthday, except that she was a sternly practical person and would certainly have asked him what she was supposed to do with it. In any case, the pearl was nearly as big as he was and he did not see how he could move it by himself.

Nat told the spider about the pearl. "Come and see," he said, "I can't move it. You could."

The spider hesitated. "That woman might come." Meaning Mrs. Dixon.

"Well, my goodness," said Nat, "if you're afraid . . . I thought you were in love."

The spider gave him a look. "Show me," he said.

They made their way down to the cooker by way of the dresser and various shadowy parts of the wall. There was no sign of Mrs. Dixon, but you never knew when she might suddenly appear. They reached the cooker, scuttled underneath, and there was the pearl, glowing in the dust and darkness.

"Nice," said the spider, "I like it." He rolled it a little with his front legs. "It's got class. Definitely. I bet my neighbour's never seen one of these. Right — let's get going." And with that he turned round and began to spin a silken net in which to carry the pearl.

A few minutes later Nat and the spider were

81

struggling back up to the top of the window with the pearl. It was hard going. The pearl was heavy; Nat had to heave from behind while the spider hauled up front. The net kept breaking and they had to stop while the spider repaired it. With much difficulty they got it up the side of the dresser, and then there was an easy flat bit where they could simply roll it from one end of the dresser to the other. But then came the sheer rise of the wall up the side of the window to the spider's home at the top. This was hard going. They struggled on valiantly, Nat pushing and the spider pulling. Rumbles and thuds from below told them that Mrs. Dixon had come into the kitchen. "Just so long as she doesn't look up," panted the spider. They felt very exposed now, on the white expanse of the wall. "She won't," said Nat, glancing backwards, "she's feeding her young."

Mrs. Dixon, at the kitchen table, spooned Heinz strained vegetables into the baby. The baby, opening and shutting his mouth, looked over her shoulder and saw a spider pulling a pearl up the wall, followed by a wood-louse. "Da!" he said.

"Yes, da . . ." said Mrs. Dixon vaguely. Conversations with babies tend to run along those lines.

And at that point the silken net broke up and the pearl fell out.

Nat and the spider heard a dreadful clatter and smash as it hit the floor. Mrs. Dixon heard nothing at all. The baby, his mouth full of strained vegetables, saw a pearl fall from the wall and waved both his hands with pleasure.

Nat and the spider peered downwards. They could just see the pearl lying on the edge of the mat beside the boiler. Mrs. Dixon got up to get something from the fridge and walked past it, her foot missing it by inches.

"Right!" said the spider grimly.

They made their way down to ground level once more. They crept along in the shadow of the skirting board and round the boiler. There they waited.

"I don't mind telling you," said the spider, "I've got the heebie-jeebies. Just sitting here looking at her."

Mrs. Dixon was idly leafing through a newspaper at the same time as pushing Heinz prunes with rice into the baby.

"Now!" said the spider.

They made a dash for the pearl. The spider started to rope it up once more. And at that moment Mrs. Dixon got up. Her enormous foot hovered above them — for an instant they thought it was all up — and then the foot passed over and on and she was standing at the cooker, doing something with a saucepan and humming to herself. The baby, though, was leaning out of his high chair and looking down at them. "Da! Da!" he said urgently to his mother.

The spider spun frantically. The pearl was netted. "Da!" cried the baby.

"Clever boy . . ." murmured Mrs. Dixon without turning round. "Yes, da . . ."

"Ssh . . ." said Nat to the baby, waving his feelers. "Not a word, eh?"

"Da," agreed the baby.

They set about it all over again. Up the dresser . . . along the top . . . up the wall. Heave and push. Pause for breath. Heave and push. I dunno, thought Nat, all this to oblige a friend. Oh well, here goes . . .

And at last they were there, above the window and outside the spider's home. The spider bustled inside, fetched a hank of cobweb and set about giving the pearl a good polish. Then he walked around it possessively. "I really go for this," he said, "it's stylish. Nobody else round here's got one of these. My neighbour's going to be hopping mad."

"Well, aren't you going to take it to your lady friend?" asked Nat, a little impatiently.

"Hm . . ." The spider patted the pearl lovingly, turned it round, gave it another polish. "You know, I ask myself if she's going to appreciate it? This is not just any old present. This is . . . unique."

"I thought she was so wonderful. I thought you wanted to marry her."

"Ah," said the spider thoughtfully, "You know one can get carried away. One can make mistakes. This has been an interesting experience. I'm having second thoughts. Truth to tell, I'm not entirely sure that one is cut out for marriage." He rolled the pearl around a little and admired his reflection in it.

"Huh!" said Nat.

The spider has been boasting about his pearl ever since. From time to time he brings it out and hangs it in the middle of his web to annoy his neighbour. If Mrs. Dixon ever looked closely at the dark and dusty place above the kitchen window she would be astonished. As for the lady spider, she had to make do with a gift-wrapped bluebottle from a more faithful admirer.

Chapter Ten

SAM, MR. DIXON'S HANDKERCHIEF, AND THE LATE-NIGHT FILM

Mr. Dixon liked to watch football on television. And why not, indeed? He liked most of all, though, to watch it late at night all on his own after Mrs. Dixon had gone up to bed, having left stern instructions about turning the lights out and locking the front door. Mr. Dixon would wait until he heard the bedroom door close, and then nip into the kitchen where he would make himself a cheese sandwich, take a can of beer from the fridge and settle blissfully on the sofa for the next hour or so.

This was annoying for the mice. By that time, they felt, the house should be theirs; the Dixons should all be asleep in bed like sensible folk and law-abiding mice should be free to go about their business undisturbed. Instead of which, there was Mr. Dixon sitting with his feet up, a can of beer in one hand and a sandwich in the other, supporting his favourite team. The mice, hungry and frustrated, would lurk crossly in the shadows until at last he switched the set off, turned the lights out and went upstairs. Occasionally he would fall asleep with the television still on, and then they had to wait even longer, until he woke up with a start, found himself facing a blank and humming screen, and took himself off. Sometimes, on these occasions, they grew tired of waiting and became rash and daring; they would dare each other to dart out and run across Mr. Dixon's sleeping feet, or play Tom Tiddler's ground on the sofa beside him.

On one such night Mr. Dixon fell into an exception-ally deep sleep. He snored. The beer can dropped from his right hand; the cheese sandwich fell from his left and lay enticingly on the sofa. The mice, becoming more and more impatient, gathered in the sitting room. The Stair mice, led by Sam, were out first.

"Dare you to pull his shoe-laces, Dad," said the eldest child.

"Don't you do any such thing," scolded Sam's wife.

Sam swaggered across the rug and nibbled a lace, quite hard. Mr. Dixon snored even louder. The mice children giggled. Sam, playing to the crowd, got onto Mr. Dixon's shoe and danced up and down. The children fell about laughing.

"Show-off!" said their mother, coldly.

Sam became even bolder. He shinned up Mr. Dixon's trouser leg and jumped from his knee to the floor. The children gasped in wonder. One of them rushed out into the hall to spread rumours of thrilling events; the other mouse families gathered in the sitting room and watched from under chairs and behind curtains.

Sam, egged on by the audience, took a nibble of Mr. Dixon's cheese sandwich.

"Hey!" someone shouted. "Give us a bite, then, Sam!" Sam flung some crumbs down and there was a merry scramble. At this point Mr. Dixon gave an enormous snore and twitched a foot. The mice scurried for cover; Sam shot behind a cushion.

Half a minute later everyone came out again. Sam, having stuffed himself on bread and cheese, threw some more down to his friends. Then, getting bored with that, he ventured gingerly onto Mr. Dixon's lap. Down below everyone held their breath. Sam wandered along Mr. Dixon's right thigh and then perched on his knee and made funny faces at the crowd below. The children shrieked encouragement. An elderly aunt muttered, "This'll end in tears, this will."

"Sam!" said his wife warningly. "You're getting above yourself."

Sam jumped across onto Mr. Dixon's other knee. He waggled his whiskers and made faces. "Go on, Dad!" yelled the children. "Do it again!"

Sam had a better idea. He returned to Mr. Dixon's lap, swarmed up his sweater and appeared on his left shoulder, waving.

At that moment someone scored a goal on the television screen. There was a roar from the crowd in Wembley, Mr. Dixon woke with a start and sat up sharply, Sam tumbled from his shoulder and dived under his handkerchief, which was lying on the sofa beside him. Down below, the other mice scuttled into the shadows and watched with bated breath.

They saw Mr. Dixon take a swig of his beer and a bite of his sandwich. Then they saw him yawn widely, pick up his handkerchief, from which the tip of Sam's tail protruded, wipe his mouth with the handkerchief and push it into his trouser pocket. There were tiny squeaks of horror.

Sam squeaked too, with terror. But by now he was deep within Mr. Dixon's pocket and wrapped up in a large red handkerchief. There was a fearful smell of matches and handkerchief and Mr. Dixon's warm leg. Ten pence pieces jingled around him. He did not dare to move. Mr. Dixon was now evidently wide awake again. His favourite team was doing nicely and Mr. Dixon was urging them towards another goal. He jiggled around on the sofa and Sam was almost smothered within the folds of the red handkerchief.

Presently Mr. Dixon became still again. After a while his head slumped against the back of the sofa and his eyes closed. Down below, the mice crept out from corners and crevices.

"Didn't I say so?" said the aunt triumphantly.

The mouse children gazed at Mr. Dixon wide-eyed, from behind a chair leg.

"Oh!" wailed the youngest. "Is this the end of father?"

"Don't talk like that," snapped Doris, but there was a quaver in her voice.

Several of the mice scrambled bravely up on to the sofa. "He's gone to sleep again," they whispered to Mr. Dixon's trouser pocket, and from deep within it Sam was heard to mutter that that wasn't going to do him much good, was it?

The mice considered the situation. Mr. Dixon's trousers were his old pair for wearing around the house, and were fairly thick but not forbiddingly so. There was only one thing to be done, and the mice set about it, with infinite caution and stealth. They began to nibble. They nibbled trouser for a few minutes, and then waited. Mr. Dixon snored gently. They nibbled some more. Inside, Sam tried to help. He nibbled at the handkerchief.

Mr. Dixon dreamed that someone was tickling him. He heaved and slapped vaguely at his side. The mice retreated; Sam, within the pocket, froze.

The mice waited. Mr. Dixon snored again. The

football match ended; the screen went blank. The mice began to nibble once more at the pocket, working in shifts, with infinite caution. Presently there was a hole the size of a small button. Sam did not dare to move. He huddled in the folds of the handkerchief, muttering to his relations, "Hurry up, can't you?"

Mr. Dixon woke up again. He stretched, yawned, saw the blank television screen and glanced at his watch. And then he got up, went into the kitchen, fetched himself another beer from the fridge, came back to the sitting room and switched on the late-night film. He took a swig of beer and settled down on the sofa once more.

Sam, during the journey to the kitchen, had almost fainted with fear. He expected Mr. Dixon's enormous hand to sweep him up, handkerchief and all, at any moment.

Once again the mice waited. And presently the combination of beer and a rather bad old film began to have their effect: Mr. Dixon sagged; his head fell back; he snored. The mice set to work.

At this moment Willie, the dog, who had been asleep in his basket in the kitchen, walked into the room. He too knew about Mr. Dixon's habit of falling asleep on the sofa and had once been able to nick his cheese sandwich. He had hoped for ever after to repeat that happy moment. Now, he observed the mice with amazement. "Here!" he said aggressively. "What do you lot think you're up to?"

"Ssh!" implored the mice.

Willie sat down. He sensed that he had them at a disadvantage. "What's up, then?"

The mice, amid mouthfuls of Mr. Dixon's polyester trousers, which did not taste all all nice, explained.

Willie laughed. "I don't know that I should sit by and do nothing. I'm a watch-dog, aren't I? I'm meant to

protect him. His trousers, too. I reckon I should wake him up."

"Please. . ." begged the mice.

"I've got my reputation to think of," said Willie. He began to growl softly. Mr. Dixon sighed and stirred.

"Please . . ." implored the mice.

"What's in it for me?" said Willie craftily.

The mice did some quick thinking. "How about we push this cheese sandwich down to you?"

"I could help myself to that," said Willie. "But all right, if you like. That'll do for starters. Then I'll have another think."

The mice heaved the cheese sandwich down onto the floor, where Willie began to eat it, wondering how else he could blackmail them.

Upstairs, Mrs. Dixon woke up. Was that the baby crying? She listened for a minute. No, the house was silent. And then she realised that the rest of the bed was empty. She frowned. She looked at her watch. It was two o'clock in the morning. Frowning dangerously now, Mrs. Dixon got out of bed and set off downstairs.

Willie was enjoying the cheese sandwich. It was Double Gloucester, his favourite. The mice were nibbling away at Mr. Dixon's pocket. Mr. Dixon was peaceably snoring. On the television screen a creature from outer space was battling with a girl in a bathing costume.

Mrs. Dixon opened the sitting room door. The mice vanished, quicker than a thought. Mr. Dixon woke, sat up with a jerk, and spilled the contents of the beer can he was holding all over himself and the sofa. Willie, his mouth full of Double Gloucester, flattened himself on the rug, ears back, tail feebly wagging. Mrs. Dixon stood there with her hands on her hips and an expression on her face that both Mr. Dixon and Willie knew all too well.

"Sorry, dear . . ." Mr. Dixon said, "I just . . ." He whipped his handkerchief out of his pocket and began to dab at the beerstains. "Whoops!" he said, as something grey and furry shot across his hand and down onto the floor.

"Good gracious," cried Mr. Dixon, "a mouse! Did you see that, dear? Of all extraordinary things, why my goodness me however did that . . ."

Mrs. Dixon glared at him. "What mouse?" she said coldly. She turned her attention to Willie. She advanced upon him.

"It's all a mistake," whined Willie. "It's not how you

think. There's been a terrible misunderstanding. Just let me explain . . ."

But it was no use. Both Mr. Dixon and Willie knew that they hadn't a leg to stand on. Mrs. Dixon had her say. At some length. She stalked around, switching off the television and locking the front door. Mr. Dixon and Willie slunk to their respective beds.

The mice came out again later and polished off one or two crumbs of the cheese sandwich that Willie had overlooked. Sam was already working on what was to become his best story after the one about how he escaped from the tea-pot. And Mrs. Dixon had some more to say, next morning, about a small, round hole in Mr. Dixon's trouser pocket.

Chapter Eleven

WILLIE, THE HAMBURGER AND THE BUS-RIDE

Willie spent most of his life sleeping, eating, thinking about eating, barking at the cat next door and getting under the Dixons' feet. It was a good life. Sometimes he was taken for a walk, which was a treat: one could roar along pulling at the lead and demand to sniff every lamp-post in the street. On the whole, though, he spent his time at Fifty-four Pavilion Road and just occasionally he felt restless. On these occasions he would lie under the hall table and wait patiently until one of the Dixons left the front door open and then he would shoot out into the street and have a little potter up and down, smelling things and looking for the next door cat. He was not supposed to do this because he was silly about cars and had nearly run under one once; sooner or later he would be missed and a Dixon, or all the Dixons, would come rushing out and yell at him to come in again. Then he would be told off, severely.

One day there was a small but busy family crisis to do with Julie Dixon pushing her brother over on the front path. The bloodshed was not great, but the noise was considerable, as well as the comings and goings as a result of which the front door was left open and unattended while Mrs. Dixon saw to plasters and peace-making.

Willie wandered out into Pavilion Road.

First of all he did what he always did, which was to

have a good smell of the nearest lamp-post, and pee over it, and then a good smell of the next one, and pee over that too. The lamp-posts all smelt different, and all were wonderfully exciting; they smelled of poodle, of spaniel, of the alsatian from the big house on the corner, and of various mixed-up dogs like Willie himself. And then there was the pavement, which was a thrilling patchwork of smells: dog and cat and spilled coke and lemonade and a whiff of Mrs. Dixon where she had paused and put her shopping basket down for a minute earlier that morning. At one point he found a wonderful place where someone had dropped an ice-cream the day before. There was quite a bit of licking to be done there, too.

He was half way down the road by now. Suddenly he remembered that he was within the territory of the alsatian on the corner, of whom he was terrified. He skulked along the wall, nervously. Was the alsatian out and about, or shut up indoors?

And then he caught sight of the cat from next door, wandering along without a care in the world. It hadn't seen him.

Willie hurled himself after the cat. He was within a yard of it before it heard him. For one brilliant moment he thought this was the day he would be able to teach it a lesson. And then the cat shot up on someone's garden wall, Willie slammed straight into the wall and almost knocked himself out, and the alsatian came out of his front gate and spotted both of them.

After that there was a minute and a half of absolute commotion. The alsatian went for Willie in a frenzy of barks and snarls. Willie howled and fled. The alsatian chased him across the road and back again and round two parked cars and a milk-float and then spotted the cat, who had been watching from the top of the wall with interest. The alsatian flung himself at the cat, and nipped its tail. The cat yowled and shot up a tree. The alsatian tried to climb the tree too, barking at full pitch. His owner came out of her house and started shouting at him.

Willie ran and ran. He looked to neither left nor right — he simply went. He was sure he could still feel the alsatian's hot breath on his tail, could hear the pad of his paws on the pavement. He ran until he was too breathless to run another yard and then he shot behind a dustbin and sat there gasping.

The street was empty. No alsatian.

Come to think of it, though, it wasn't any street he'd ever seen before, either. Willie came out from behind the dustbin and looked around. Interesting. New place, new smells. He pottered along busily. He found half a sausage roll and ate it; he snuffed for a long time at a place where a dachshund had been sitting half an hour before.

He wandered on.

Now he was in another street: a busy street with people and shops. This was even more interesting. Willie went up to several people to say hello and ask if by any chance they had any chocolates or biscuits on them that they didn't want. Most of them took no notice of him but one girl patted him and Willie told her that he hadn't had any breakfast or any supper the night before come to that and he lived with some cruel people who kept him shut in a cupboard all the time. The little girl appeared not to understand this but she gave him what was left of a boiled sweet she had been sucking; Willie gulped that down and padded off to try his luck elsewhere.

There was the most exquisite smell. Hamburger! A smell Willie knew well. Very occasionally he got the end of a hamburger that no one could finish up at home at Pavilion Road. Not often enough, in his opinion. And here, he now saw, was a place into which people walked and were handed hamburgers by the plateful. Dogs, also?

He trotted into the Macdonalds behind an elderly man who went and sat down at a table. Willie sat at his feet, making himself look as small and obliging as possible. Then he looked around hopefully.

A woman who was whisking about with dirty plates said, "No dogs!" loudly and sternly. Willie, naturally, paid no attention.

"No dogs, sir!" said the woman even more loudly to the elderly man, who was reading a newspaper.

"Hamburger and chips, please, miss," he said.

"I'm sorry, sir, but you can't bring your dog in here," said the woman sternly.

"I haven't got a dog," snapped the man. "I don't like dogs, do I? It's cats I've got."

"Then whose is that dog?" demanded the woman, who didn't like his tone.

She pointed triumphantly at Willie, but Willie was no longer there. Seeing that there was a problem of some kind he had slipped quietly off under the tables and was now on the far side of the room where he had spotted a baby in a high-chair. Babies in high-chairs drop things — food, usually. The woman and the man continued to argue.

The baby, sure enough, dropped a rusk, which Willie ate gratefully. It leaned over the edge of its chair and offered a finger to Willie. Willie stood up on his hind legs and licked the finger: he was fond of babies.

At that point the baby's mother caught sight of Willie and made loud shooing noises. The woman broke off her argument, also saw Willie, and came marching over. "Out!" she shouted. "Get outside, you!" She poked at Willie with a foot, Willie dodged. The woman seized a newspaper and flapped it at him with her free hand; in the other she was carrying two plates of half-eaten hamburger and peas, with another one lodged half way up her arm.

Willie didn't like having newspapers flapped at him. He decided to leave in a dignified manner. He headed for the door. The woman was right in his way, so he aimed straight between her feet.

The woman tripped. The three plates of hamburgers and peas went flying. A chewed hamburger landed directly in front of Willie who came to an abrupt stop. How kind. So they did hand out hamburgers to dogs also. Why hadn't they said so in the first place, then? He seized the largest hamburger. It occurred to him as he did so that there was a disagreeable amount of shouting and rushing around going on now and it might be more peaceful to eat it outside, so he took a firm grip on it and bolted into the street.

He ate the hamburger peacefully underneath a tree

a little way away. It was excellent. He licked his lips. What one really needed now was a nice saucer of milk to round things off. Perhaps it was time to go home and see if Mrs. Dixon was feeling in a generous mood.

Home?

Where was home?

Willie looked up and down the street. He hadn't the slightest idea where he was. There were cars everywhere, and motorbikes, and bicycles, and people — and they were all cars and motorbikes and people that he didn't know. He panicked. He began to rush around looking for Mrs. Dixon, for Mr. Dixon — for any Dixon at all. He dashed up to people sniffing furiously to see if they smelled at all of Dixon: none of them did.

Willie sat down outside a branch of Marks and Spencer and howled. "Lost!" he howled. "Abandoned and homeless! Take me home and look after me! Fetch the RSPCA!"

People stopped to stare at him. Willie's purpose had been to attract attention and he had certainly succeeded. Those who did not like dogs muttered about how disgraceful it was that there were these strays all over the place and it was time the government did something about it. Those who did like dogs made friendly noises at Willie and said it was a shame. Someone offered him a piece of chocolate but he was so full of hamburger that he simply couldn't face it. It was the first time in his life he had ever refused anything in the food line. The thought of this made him feel even more desperate. "I can't even eat! I'm ill! Help me!"

Suddenly Willie found himself swept up into the air. A large woman with a red face had picked him up and tucked him under one arm, explaining to the crowd that she kept an Animal Sanctuary and would see that the poor little chap found a nice home. Willie did not follow this; all he knew was that he was clamped uncomfortably under the woman's arm and that he wasn't at all sure he liked her. She didn't smell right; she didn't smell at all like Mrs. Dixon. He struggled. The woman gripped him even more firmly and began to walk away.

Just then he saw Mrs. Dixon. The back of Mrs. Dixon. Quite a long way away. Looking in the window of Boots the Chemist.

Willie wriggled desperately. He kicked and scrabbled. The woman dropped him and he bolted off towards Mrs. Dixon.

He reached her just before she went into Boots. He hurled himself at her, wagging and whimpering — and it wasn't Mrs. Dixon at all. She didn't like dogs, either. She said so, loudly.

Willie sat on the pavement and the not-Mrs.-Dixon went into Boots, still saying unpleasant things. Willie was about to start howling again when a bus drew up at the stop nearby and a group of people waiting began to get onto it. One of them was Mrs. Dixon. Oh, definitely she was Mrs. Dixon.

He shot onto the bus behind her and under one of the seats. The bell rang and the bus moved off. Willie sniffed fondly at Mrs. Dixon's legs and immediately realised that this wasn't her either. The world was full of imitation Mrs. Dixons, it seemed. He was sitting beside the leg of a totally strange woman. And furthermore he was on a bus which was lurching off to goodness knows where and evidently he wasn't welcome in any case; everyone was looking at him, voices were raised, a hand descended towards him . . .

Willie made for the platform. The bus slowed down at a corner and Willie jumped off.

The busy shopping street had been left behind. This was a quieter place, with houses not unlike those in Pavilion Road and not many people around. Willie sat down, panting. Being lost was the most exhausting thing he had ever known. In fact, now he came to think about it, he was even beginning to feel slightly hungry again. He sniffed; somewhere, in one of those houses, someone was having a delicious fry-up. Bangers and bacon. Willie licked his lips.

He sniffed some more. Air, for dogs, is a fascinating soup of assorted smells. Apart from the bangers and bacon Willie could smell petrol, smoke, cat, a woman mowing her lawn further down the road, roses, an old chicken leg in a rubbish bin beside him and — far away behind and beyond all this — something else.

There was a whiff — the faintest whiff — of home. Of Fifty-four Pavilion Road. Of the Dixons.

He sniffed and sniffed. He trotted off in one direction and sniffed some more. No, it had got fainter. He

turned round and trotted off the other way, with his nose to the pavement now. And he picked up a stale and long-ago but distinct trace of Mrs. Dixon. Sometime, yesterday maybe, or the day before, Mrs. Dixon had walked along here.

Willie rushed on, panting and snuffing. He lost the smell altogether and then he found it again and then he lost it once more. He crashed into someone walking their spaniel. The spaniel flew around on the end of its lead barking; Willie paid no attention at all but hurried on. He went right past a tabby cat grooming itself on a doorstep. The cat tore up a fence and sat on top shouting rude things but Willie was too busy to answer back. He turned a corner into another street . . . and it was Pavilion Road.

He galloped the last hundred yards. He bolted in at the open front door and into the kitchen, where Mrs. Dixon and the children were having tea.

Willie flung himself into Mrs. Dixon's lap, knocking her cup of tea out of her hand and putting muddy blobs from his feet all over her skirt. "I'm starving!" he wailed. "I've been lost for a week and I've had nothing to eat and I'm worn out and a woman tried to kidnap me! And I'm pleased to see you again even if you don't take care of me properly and you let me get lost and you don't feed me properly and . . ."

Willie continued thus while Mrs. Dixon scolded and told him to stop barking and jumping and said to the children that she couldn't imagine what on earth was wrong with the dog.

For the fact was that no one had noticed Willie was missing.

This is not really the end of the story; it is the beginning, in a sense.

Such things are going on up and down the country, in thousands of other houses like Fifty-four Pavilion Road. Houses that you wouldn't look at twice if you were passing in a bus or a car. It's as well the papers have never got on to it: there'd be a national scandal. And how do I know so much about it? Well, like Mrs. Dixon, I have come across the occasional wood-louse in my bath, or the odd piece of nibbled cheese in my kitchen, and have realised that I was sharing my home with others, like it or not. And since I am partial to stories, it occurred to me that these creatures no doubt had a few tales to tell, just as most people do.

I wonder what is going on in your house?